THE OTHER SIDE OF SOBER

Hell's slippery slope

Elsie J.M. Page

April 5, 2018
To Olivia
Blue skys &
Pleasant memories
E. Joyce M. Page.

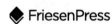 FriesenPress

Suite 300 - 990 Fort St
Victoria, BC, V8V 3K2
Canada

www.friesenpress.com

ISBN
978-1-5255-1593-4 (Hardcover)
978-1-5255-1594-1 (Paperback)
978-1-5255-1595-8 (eBook)

1. FICTION, BIOGRAPHICAL

Distributed to the trade by The Ingram Book Company

ACKNOWLEDGMENTS

To the special people in my life who generously supported
and encouraged me to keep on writing and freely offered good advice.
Thanks to Faye and Ken Vryenhoek, Lavaine Lightbown, and of course, my
son, James.

A very special thank you to my lifelong friend
Sophie Vera Huebert
for all her advice, spell checking, proofreading and support.
Without you, this story would remain untold.

I dedicate this story to James III, Rothelle,
Marlene, Russ, Tyler, Richard, Brett
and everyone who is trying to find their way in life.
May your choices be wise, safe, and sober,
and may your world be filled with
happiness, courage, faith, hope
and
free of addictions.

Books written by Elsie J.M. Page

Sacrifice of love

Unlucky half sister

The other side of sober

PROLOGUE

Genre – Biographical/Fiction
Names of people and places have been changed to protect the innocent

JESSIE MCGANN'S STRICT METHODIST UPBRINGING DIDN'T PREPARE HER FOR a world of drinking, gambling, greed, manipulating, and questionable ethics. It was a fluke of fate that slid the handsome young Willie Masterson into her overprotected life, and she found herself on a slippery downhill slide in a world of addictions that he cunningly concealed until after they were married. She faced the challenges of life with courage and determination and became Willie's reliable rescuer, leaning post, and door mat. This enabled him to concentrate on destroying both their lives, in the cruelest fashion. Willie was generous with his time and money, to a fault, which bought him many fair-weather friends who took advantage of him in subtle ways he was too blind to see. He loved his children, and provided them with all the necessities of life, and more. Jessie knew she couldn't leave her troublesome marriage. She couldn't provide the children she loved so dearly, with the comforts of a home, music, education, and sports they now enjoyed, so she placed her needs and desires on the back burner of life. As her golden years unfolded, she found the strength and courage to make several major life changes. Willie had stopped drinking and she believed he was cured of this nasty illness. Little did she know that alcoholics are never cured. They suffer from a disease of excuses, and they simply move to another addiction that continues to mess up their life. Jessie bravely walked away, this time for good. She opened a new door and found unexpected happiness in the palm of her hand.

THE OTHER SIDE OF SOBER

Hell's slippery slope

Elsie J.M. Page

I married an alcoholic. Oh, I didn't do it intentionally. Anyone, with an ounce of brains wouldn't do such a thing. I didn't know what an alcoholic was, or how deceptive and destructive one could be, to themselves, and to those they love. Let me tell you how my life unfolded.

I'm Jessie, child number ten, in the household of David and Martha McGann. My parents are strict Methodists, loving and overprotective. There were household rules I must adhere to at all cost. Besides no smoking or drinking, I must be home every evening before sundown, and during the winter months that was rather early. However, if I wanted to go skiing, skating, or other outdoor winter sports, I was allowed a little slack.

Although I was eighteen years old, I wasn't into serious dating . . . yet. It's not that I was an ugly duckling, no, I was just 'plain Jane' Jessie. Young suitors shied away from me because of all my life's restrictions. Boys considered me no fun at all, but that didn't bother me as I had plenty of fun just being me. I inherited a touch of Irish humor that I used generously on friends and family. Although my parents never told me, I knew I was loved and cherished. Our home was full of laughter, friends, music and song, and respect. I knew I was Daddy's favorite, but I was the only one still living at home. All my siblings were working out of town.

Our home was nestled in a beautiful suburban part of Winnipeg, Manitoba, amid two acres of fertile land that was outlined with tall lilac bushes that perfumed the air each spring. The back half of our acreage housed a tiny chicken house and essential garden space. The front half displayed our home, where tall maple, ash and oak trees provided summer shade, and Mother Martha rose bushes that beautified her flower gardens. Our house wasn't fancy, but it was large and homey, with a door that was never locked, and friends were always welcome.

Daddy had an enlarged heart and a severe case of asthma that would erupt whenever he tried to lift or carry anything. Because of the dust factor, he was unable to return to his 'Furniture Redesigning and Upholstering' profession, so Mother Martha and I kept the home fire burning. I took care of the outdoor chores, like cleaning the chicken poop off the roosts and sprinkling them with lime, putting down fresh straw once a week, filling the water troughs daily, cutting wood and carrying in coal for indoor use, emptying the "honey pail" (pee pot) and many more incidentals. Mother Martha did the cooking, cleaning, laundry and caring for Daddy, as well as garden work and sales. I was strong and healthy, and happy to help my parents in any way I could.

"The lucky guy that dates me has to be tall, dark and handsome, with a mouthful of white teeth, no acne and no whiskers," I proudly told my parents. "It's okay if he doesn't have money, I don't have any either. That will make us equal on a slippery slope," I giggled, as I filled the wood box to capacity to last the night. "I just hope he isn't lazy, and can play the bagpipes like you used to do, before you got sick, Daddy. I'll try my best to pick a good mate that you will approve of, and maybe even love." Daddy simply gave me an adoring smile.

With all the restrictions laid down by my overprotective parents, I was surprised to be invited to a toboggan party special event, in Sears Shopping Mall parking lot.

The boy inviting me was acne king Steven Pointer. He was a nice kid from my night school class, who had possession of his own teeth and no whiskers, so I considered two out of three a good average. He didn't own a car, so plans were made to meet on the Red River Motor Coach bus that made a daily trip into City Central at 7:00 p.m. and a return trip at midnight. I was well equipped with parka, mitts, moccasins, and well insulated ski pants. It was -25 below zero, so not much could go wrong on this date. I could go.

Steven was a real gentleman, he even saved me a seat on the bus. He was dressed for the occasion in a complete snowmobile suit and a big smile. We chatted happily all the way to the Mall.

It was a bitterly cold January night, with a nasty wind, but we climbed the steep icy steps to the top of the fifty-foot slide, along with all the other party hardy teens. The toboggan was huge. It held ten passengers . . . maybe more, but there was a mad scramble for who got on and who was left behind. It was totally out of control. Steven and I managed to fight our way on, but the teens were pushing and shunting and moving everyone back, as more and more tried to pile on board.

The man in charge announced that everyone must wrap their feet around the person in front of them, and put their arms around their waist. This was to insure no one fell off or got hurt, as the ride was steep and fast.

With all the shuffling and clamoring for space, Steven was pushed off the end of the toboggan. I tried to free myself to join him, but the fellow in front of me held my legs tight and refused to let go. I think he liked the feel of my insulated ski pants. There's no way he could feel my legs under all the padding.

"Let me go," I shouted, as loud as I could over the noisy crowd, but the fellow seated in front of me just laughed and chose to ignore my predicament and held my legs all the tighter.

I was seated firmly on the icy surface of the slide when the men in charge gave the toboggan a mighty push and the toboggan went flying, with my buttocks dragging and bumping along the slippery slope. I thought this was extremely funny, but when the toboggan stopped halfway to the returning slide, and another one was coming down behind us at top speed, it wasn't so funny. Everyone quickly rolled over into the snow to avoid the crash. The fellow who was holding my legs helped me out of the knee-deep snowdrift and we started walking to the return slide, but the wind was so bitterly cold, everyone decided to duck into the coffee shop at the Mall instead.

I glanced over to see if Steven was on the ride that went flying by, but he wasn't there. I wasn't too concerned, as I had my return bus fare safely tucked away, and I knew he knew his way home.

The whole toboggan load ended up in the toasty warm coffee shop. Coffee was ordered all around and the fellow who had held my legs offered to buy me coffee, but I refused to allow him the privilege. I thought he was trying to pick me up and I wasn't interested, although he was good looking, with blonde curly hair, a good set of white teeth and no whiskers. That was two out of three . . . not a bad average.

I reached for the sugar jar *(which had a large pouring spout)* and proceeded to pour sugar into my coffee cup. The lid had been purposely loosened and the whole bottle of sugar dumped into my cup. Roars of laughter filled the room. Apparently, that was something teens did for kicks. I turned red from embarrassment. Gritting my teeth, and with my nose held high, I ordered a fresh cup of coffee. I needed it to warm my body and cool my tongue.

The leg holder fellow looked at me and smiled. "My name is Willie Masterson, and what's yours?" he asked in a quiet tone.

I said, "Jessie." That was it. No more information was going to escape my lips.

"It's a very cold night. Can I drive you home?" Willie asked.

To this he received a very soft, polite, "No!"

"Can I see you tomorrow?" he persisted.

"Sorry, but I work at Zellers during the day, and go to night school in the evening.

I have no time for dates," I replied rather aloof. "This is an unusual outing for me."

"I could meet you after night school and drive you home," he persisted.

A spark of interest was smoldering, but I refused to fan the flame. "If you want to meet me after night school, you can wait for me at the school door. I'll be out at 9:30 p.m. Don't be late. I wait for no one. I have a bus to catch, and there's only one leaving at that hour of the night, so I can't afford to miss it. If you aren't there when I come down, I'll be on my way."

"I'll be there," he said with a winning boyish smile.

Night school was over, and I checked to see if Willie really came. He wasn't there. I wasn't surprised . . . I didn't exactly encourage the poor fellow.

I caught my bus and went home feeling a little guilty. I could have waited five minutes.

The next day I received a phone call at work. It was Willie.

"I waited two hours in the bitter cold for you to come out of night school last evening, and you didn't show. Finally, the principal came out, and was locking the building for the night, and he told me you left long ago. I may have been two or three minutes late, but no more. Couldn't you wait a couple of minutes to see if I was perhaps tied up in traffic?" he scolded.

Now I felt like a heel. When he asked to see me again, I simply had to give in. We met at the bus depot, had coffee, and chatted. He was very nice, I must admit. I tried to show interest in what he was saying and struggled to keep the conversation alive.

"Where do you work," I asked . . . just to be polite, as I really didn't care. He told me the name of some company I'd never heard of, and I wasn't the least bit interested in.

"Do you like fish?" he asked.

"Oh yes," I said, finding the subject rather boring.

"What kind of fish do you like?" he inquired.

Now I was in trouble! I said I liked fish, so now what could I tell him. I had to think fast. What is the name of a fish? The only one I could think of was salmon. *(Right, it comes in a can.)*

I stated my fish preference and the subject was closed until the next meeting.

I was at the bus depot after night school as usual, when along came Willie with a huge frozen salmon, about four feet long. "Here," he said. "I hope you enjoy this salmon . . . it's a sockeye," like I should know what that was.

I was speechless, which was rather unusual for me. What was I going to do with this darn fish? How could I explain to my parents that a perfect stranger gave it to me? Maybe I could say I found it on the sidewalk. No, I don't think that would work. I was in a tizzy. Being from a rather humble home, I respected the value of food. My conscience wouldn't allow me to throw it in the garbage. I boarded the toasty warm bus and settled in for the half hour ride home. The fish started to melt, and before I left the bus there was a puddle of stinky fish water on the floor by my seat. I exited quickly at my stop.

Daddy David was in bed sleeping when I tiptoed into the kitchen. I called mother and told her the truth. "I don't know what to do, Mom. What will I tell Daddy?" I was terrified that I was in big trouble, but as usual, mother came to the rescue. She lit the kerosene lamp so the fish would be more visible before calling her sleeping husband. Mother Martha shook him from a sound sleep. "Dave, come to the kitchen. There's something you have to see."

Daddy David was annoyed! "What the heck is so interesting in the darn kitchen at this hour of the night." he grumbled.

"Just you come and see. There's a big surprise for you. Someone has sent you a wonderful present. You have to get up to see it."

"Who the heck would send me a present?" daddy muttered, but he slowly rolled out of bed and wandered into the dimly lit kitchen in his long underwear. *(At least he was well covered)*

Even in the flickering lamplight, daddy David could see the fish that stretched across the kitchen table. He was fascinated. "What a wonderful specimen this is!" he exclaimed. "I can't believe it! Who would send me a fish like this?"

With trembling lips, I quickly added to mother's story. "I met a fellow at work and he said he owned a fish company. I told him my father loved fish, and he brought this one for you."

"Well, I'll have to meet this fellow and thank him. It sure is a beauty," he said as he inspected every scale on the poor fish, admiring its perfection for a long time before returning to his bedroom.

Having escaped that problem, I breathed a sigh of relief and went to bed and slept soundly.

***

If you really want to find someone, it's not difficult. Willie knew my first name and where I worked. With a little ingenuity, he managed to find where I lived. Sunday morning, he drove in our yard in his shiny black Lincoln Continental. I nearly died on the spot. I turned forty shades of red when I greeted him at the door. I invited him in and said, "Daddy, this is the gentleman who sent you the fish." Then I took off out the door and busied myself sweeping snow from the doorstep and pathway.

The two men talked forever! I couldn't believe how well they got along. Mother made tea and I felt obligated to join them. It was an uncomfortable visit for me, but Willie was at ease and my parents were delighted with the well-dressed gentleman, and the expensive car he drove. After tea was over, Willie left and waved a cheery goodbye, as much as to say, 'I made it to first base.'

Willie realized I was working hard during the day, plus attending a night school accounting course, and gave me some space. Now I was wondering why he wasn't contacting me, but was delighted that he had enough brains to not interrupt my busy schedule. He stopped by the bus depot a couple of times and we had coffee and a short chat before I had to leave, but every Sunday morning he was at my door again. Daddy was sure he was coming for another hour - long conversation about his chickens, and how many eggs he got per hen, per week. Willie was obviously trying to impress Daddy, and asked, "How many eggs did the roosters lay per week?" That won Daddy's heart. He laughed so hard his one glass eye nearly popped out of its socket.

I didn't have to worry about entertaining Willie because my dad was more than willing to do the job. *(Bless you Daddy!)* Willie was slowly becoming part of the family.

Then the big moment came! Willie invited me to a party at his friend's house. I don't know who the party was for. It was somebody's wife's cousin's divorce party, or something like that. I could go to this event with Willie because he gave Daddy that darn fish. *(Daddy got the fish but I got the hook)*

I found a convenient corner to sit, sort of out of the way of the smokers and drinkers. I wasn't impressed with the lot, and I had to keep blowing my nose and wiping my burning eyes from the smoke in the room. Willie snuggled up close beside me and took my Kleenex-free hand in his. He seemed proud to have me there. I don't know why, because I fit in like a glove with six thumbs. Before the night was over he whispered in my ear – "Will you marry me?"

I looked at him in surprise and said, "Ya right! Maybe next year on the ice!" He reached over and hugged me, like it was the answer he was hoping for. Finally, the party ended and we escaped to where there was more oxygen and less noise. He drove me home.

The following week Willie invited me to visit his grandma. She lived in a small town called Saddle Creek, MB. I thought it was nice to meet his grandmother because I didn't have one. Mine were both dead before I was born. The thought of meeting a grandmother and having a nice car ride in the country was appealing – and getting out of work at home was a bonus. Once again, I could go with the fish man.

Grandma was as cute as a pickle. She spoke perfect broken English with a Dutch accent. Her home was small, neat, clean, and interesting. She had homemade rugs all over her house that were expertly braided from rags. Framed needlepoint pictures adorned the walls in several places. Crocheted doilies were placed appropriately on the furniture. The floors throughout the home were covered with linoleum, well-worn in places, but spotlessly clean. She had a large well-kept yard, a big vegetable garden and a collie dog. She lived alone.

The first thing she offered us was tea. *(That was something my mother would do.)* Tea and cookies loaded with raisins . . . and I absolutely hate raisins. To be polite, I swallowed them whole and washed them down with tea, then she insisted on reading my tea leaves.

"I see a wedding," she said, among other things . . . like a letter, a surprise visitor, money, the usual garbage. But the word 'wedding' struck me as rather cute from the old lady. Perhaps she hoped her grandson would marry someone as great as me. *(Way to go grandma)*

After lunch, we played cards. Grandma was an expert at cheating. She wore a big white apron with large pockets that somehow managed to contain all the aces. It was so entertaining. We laughed and laughed, and grandma had a ball winning all the games against us city slickers.

Next, it was supper time. How she managed to find so many things I didn't like was amazing. Parsnips, vegetable marrow, turnips, squash, liver, and for dessert she really topped the list. She served sliced bananas and cream. She batted 100, but she was so darn cute I ate it all. I just didn't chew any of it. I cut everything in tiny chunks and washed it down with tea.

I survived the visit, and we headed home for some Milk of Magnesia for my upset tummy.

A few weeks later, Willie invited me to his home for dinner. Holy cow! I'd never been invited to anyone's house for dinner before, but I had strict upbringing regarding table manners, so I wasn't really alarmed. I could handle it. I learned to handle a lot of difficult situations in my lifetime . . . this one should be a piece of cake. It seemed my leash got a lot longer when Willie the fish man was around, so off I went.

The first shock was, Willie's family home was a BIG fancy one, sprawling across a huge well-kept lawn that draped itself down to the rivers edge. Second shock, his family was also big, and they were all there, and every eye was on me. I felt like I was being scrutinized and anatomized. There was a definite coolness in the air. The dining room table was elegantly set with English bone china dishes, all matching and harboring no chips or cracks. They were accompanied by sterling silver cutlery and snow white lacy table napkins. Crystal glasses sparkled brightly from the light of the massive overhead chandelier.

Willie took my arm and led me to my seating place. Once everyone was settled, the wine and whiskey was poured. Everyone's glass was filled, even the glasses of the three young children who looked no more than twelve to fourteen years of age. Mr. Masterson proposed a toast to the honored guest . . .that was me.

At first, I didn't realize he was toasting me. Each member of the family raised their glass of liquor and looked at me to do the same. I picked up my water glass and joined the celebration.

"You must drink your wine for good luck," Willie's mother instructed.

"I'm sorry, but I don't drink liquor. I'm quite happy with water, thank you," I explained as politely as I could. A chorus of laughter from Willie's parents and six siblings, filled the room.

"I can see you have no class, no culture my dear," Mrs. Masterson said, as she downed a mouthful of spirits with the elegance of a queen.

I choked down a lovely dinner, and immediately after the meal I proceeded to clear away the dishes. I wanted to make a good impression. Heck, I was good at washing dishes. I got right to it. In no time at all I had them done and was wiping down the counter when I came across a five-pound pail of slop water. 'Hmm,' I said to myself. 'I wonder what I should do with this? Would they flush this down the toilet?' We didn't have running water in our house, so I wasn't sure what you could throw in that fancy facility. I thought I'd better ask Willie's mother before I did something stupid.

"Where should I throw this dirty water?" I asked in all sincerity.

His mother gave me the strangest look, and said with disgust, "Those are the oysters my dear!" and unceremoniously removed the can from my hard-working hands. I knew at that precise moment I had not impressed this family.

After the cleanup was done, everyone sat around talking and smoking. Abstaining was not overlooked by the family.

"I see we have to teach you some much needed social etiquette," Willie's mother announced to the coolness in the room.

The subject of marriage came up casually by Willie's father, who seemed anxious to discuss it.

"So, I hear you two are getting married," he stated.

"Oh, not for a long time! At least a year," I replied in earnest.

Willie's mother jumped out of her chair, swinging her finger back and forth in front of my nose. She spoke with an authoritative, over dignified voice, "You are getting married on the 1st of December. I spoke to the minister and the church is booked. You can't change it now. It's all settled."

I went into partial cardiac arrest. If silence is golden, then this was likely a twenty-one-karat gold moment. I was afraid to speak because I knew if I opened my mouth it wouldn't be pretty, and I'd be walking home.

Willie wasn't saying anything, and the trip home was more than uneventful. It was miserably quiet. I couldn't believe his mother would take it upon herself to arrange my marriage without my consent. Willie must have given his permission. (*Nice guy!*) I waited until he pulled into my yard before I opened the floodgate.

"What the hell are these wedding arrangements about?" Before he had a chance to answer, I added, "May I remind you, I said maybe next year . . . with emphasis on maybe! Next year doesn't arrive on the calendar in six months . . . not in my orbit. I have no money for a wedding and neither does my family. I have other priorities I plan to take care of, long before I ever think of marriage.

"What are the priorities?" Willie asked in a hurt, meek little voice.

"I'm saving my money to buy a piano. That comes under the heading of first!"

"I'll buy you a piano after we get married, and don't worry about the cost of the wedding. My parents will pay for everything. That's no problem. All my father's business associates will be invited to attend and he will want to impress them with a fancy wedding. I asked my mom to make the arrangements because I will be leaving to go up north to our fishing camp at the end of May, and I'll be gone till late fall. I'll be at home till the winter fishing starts. I was hoping to get married before that. I don't want to lose you. I love you with all my heart. I even bought you this," and he reached inside his pocket and produced a beautiful engagement ring. He took my left hand and slid the sparkling ring on my finger. Silvery moonlight cast its shadowy glow across the car window and onto my trembling hand. I just stared in silent wonder at the beautiful diamond, trying to place which fairy-tale world I was lost in. I was speechless! He grabbed me and kissed me so hard my lips blistered. We were both crying and laughing and blubbering hysterically. I was unsure of my sanity, but mesmerized by the glittering gem on my finger. Willie had an answer for each problem I tried to put forth. "Don't worry about a single thing my darling," he said. "I will take care of everything. What I can't do, my parents will take care of."

My parents were delighted with the news. They thought Willie was closely related to God, and therefore a perfect match for me.

We were to be married on December 1, as was dictated by the Masterson family.

***

Much to my surprise, a group of Masterson friends and relatives held a bridal shower for me. Willie transported me to and from the joyful occasion. All the ladies attending were friends and relatives of Willie's parents. It was a happy-go-lucky celebration for everyone, except me. Most of the conversations were held in what seemed to be a Dutch language, so I had no clue what was being discussed. The body language and laughter made me uncomfortable. One lady took pity and spoke to me in English. She said, "I hope you know how lucky you are. Willie could have married anyone in the world he wanted. The family are disappointed that he didn't choose to marry Gracie, the family's long-time friend. Of course, Grace would love to be walking in your shoes today." With these words of wisdom, she turned to converse with another lady, in Dutch.

I fought back tears and forced my way through the day with as much dignity as I could muster.

We received tons of useless wedding gifts that were lovely to look at. There were silver tea services, silver candle holders, silver trimmed plates and glasses, silver cutlery, everything was silver, you name it, all needing cleaning and polishing more often than my teeth. I had them earmarked for the Good Will in the future, but I was grateful for all the gifts that poured in from the family, friends, and business associates. As poor as I was, I managed to keep everything I owned, color coordinated. We were now the proud owners of a brown carpet, red and purple towels, green chesterfield, yellow padded chrome table and chairs, wine colored rocking chair and green and beige drapes. The rainbow of gifts did nothing for my taste buds, but it was a start for our future life together. I accepted them graciously and counted my blessings.

One special gift I received from my future mother-in-law, was a coffee bag. She made coffee in a dirty brown bag that resembled an old man's work sock. It was attached to a sieve handle and rim. She thought I needed one of these fancy appliances. I wasn't impressed with the look of this dirty looking bag, but reserved my thoughts. 'If I must have a rag bag coffee maker, it wasn't going to be stained and ugly,' I mentally noted. Before I used it, I bleached it.

The first coffee I served, tasted, and smelled of Javex. My company bitterly complained about the terrible taste of the coffee. I was positive this was just another cruel insult they were adding to my already fragile feelings. One of the ladies got up to inspect my coffee maker and discovered the problem. When I mentioned how I cleaned the bag, they had a good laugh at my expense, and explained to stupid little me, that you had to boil the bag in coffee to make it brown. Once the bag was 'cured' the coffee was excellent. This was my first lesson in kitchen duties, much to the disgust of future family members.

The wedding day arrived, and it was a regular December day in 1951, with snowflakes floating from the sky. They were large and beautiful and clung to my velvet wedding gown. Cheap confetti were thrown at me, and my wedding gown became polka-dotted with every color of a rainbow. I rushed to the bathroom to wash my dress in the sink. I had the first dance with Willie in a soaking wet gown. My floor length veil helped to mask the embarrassing problem.

The wedding was elegant, I suppose, but a little strange. There were three hundred guests, but the only people I knew besides Willie's family, was my mother, my maid of honor and two bridesmaids. Daddy was ill and couldn't attend. I didn't invite any of my friends and relatives as I wasn't paying for the wedding, and I didn't want to take advantage of the Masterson's generosity.

I went through the motions, following instructions, and being coached by family members.

The evening eventually came to an end for Willie and me. Everyone cheered as we left the hall and I could breathe freely once again. The invited guests remained and continued drinking and dancing to the music of a wonderful orchestra, while we headed for our honeymoon suite in a well known upscale hotel. I was now a married woman, living in a fantasy world. Nothing seemed real. I wasn't happy, and I wasn't sad. I don't know what I was feeling. Perhaps it was fear of the unknown.

The next day, we left on our honeymoon, by Greyhound bus. Destination – Niagara Falls.

***

Our first overnight stay was Chicago. We booked into a huge hotel, but before retiring we looked up a long-lost cousin who happened to live nearby. We invaded their space and they were great hosts, serving delicious food and plenty to drink. This was the first time I saw Willie drunk. I was not impressed. At first, he slurred in his speech, then he acted funny and a bit silly, but after a lengthy and interesting visit we made it back to the hotel where he passed out for the night. I couldn't sleep. I wasn't happy with this inebriated body lying next to me . . . and he stunk of liquor. I lay awake for hours, listening to my beloved husband snore.

In the early morning hours, I heard someone trying our door. I froze in fear! We were on the fifteenth floor of this hotel, and to me it felt like outer space. I could hear two men talking and they sounded like Willie looked . . . plastered. Their key wouldn't work, thank goodness, but the one fellow suggested to his partner that he climb through the open hinged window over the door. I freaked out at this point and shook Willie as hard as I could, but he wouldn't wake up. Then I pounded him. He sweet-dreamed to the loving beat of my fists. I finally realized I was on my own. I went to the door and shouted, "You've got the wrong suite! Go away! This is not your room!" They mumbled some profanity and moved on. I collapsed beside my inebriated life protector.

The following day, I notified my sister and brother in Toronto that we would be dropping by on our way to Niagara Falls. This was thrilling for me, as I hadn't seen my sister and brother since I was a tiny tot, and didn't really know what they looked like. I had nothing to go on but a couple of faded black and white, well-worn pictures.

Sister Dolly Donnahue said she would meet us at the bus depot. We got off the bus and I looked around for someone that might resemble my family, but didn't recognize anyone. We decided to take a taxi to Dolly's house. No one was home. We sat on the doorstep with our suitcases, and long faces. About an hour later, Dolly and her husband Grant came home. She knew it had to be me on the doorstep, and said as she jumped out of the car, "I was looking for someone who was short and fat. You aren't fat!" She rushed into my arms and hugged me gently and I could instantly feel her sisterly warmth. I loved Dolly, immediately . . . all 113 pounds of me. It was a grand reunion. Dolly was a plump, jolly person. She loved to cook, and had plenty of fancy foods and desserts to serve us. She offered household tips, and I hungrily absorbed her advice, because I didn't know how to cook.

Her home was tiny, tastefully decorated, neat, spotlessly clean, and comfortable. The first thing I noticed was her piano. I couldn't take my eyes from it. "Willie promised me a piano," I said with confidence. "I can hardly wait. I have longed for a piano all my life."

Dolly showed me how her piano could play by itself. I was fascinated watching the keys jump up and down as wonderful music filled the room. I sat on the bench and pretended I was playing, and she laughed and gave me another big hug. "It's not a home if it doesn't have music in it," she chuckled. "I know you will enjoy your piano when you get it."

Grant was a homely duck, but a jolly fellow who loved to play tricks on the unsuspecting. His next-door neighbor was on vacation and Grant thought it was a perfect time to pull a prank. The neighbor had a pear tree that never produced any fruit and he constantly complained about this, to anyone who would listen. While he was away, Grant purchased a half dozen green pears and asked Willie to help him wire them to the tree, even if it was out of season. Then the two men found a comfortable chair where they enjoyed a few beers, exchanging friendly conversation, as they got tipsy. Dolly and I were not impressed, but we found interesting things to do in the kitchen. She was a marvelous cook and had a 'Helpful Hints' column in the Globe and Mail newspaper. I was impressed and asked a lot of questions.

The visit was short, but wonderful. We hugged and kissed and hugged again. Parting was difficult, but we had to leave.

The following day we went to meet my oldest brother, Gregory McGann, who was two years younger than Dolly. He lived about an hour away, if you were traveling at excessive speed on the 401. He was a delightful sort. He lifted me off my feet in a bear hug, and held me there till my sides were sore. He had a house full of kids and a happy little wife, and a welcome mat as big as Texas. He showed us around his home, which included a basement full *(I mean wall to wall)* of car and motorcycle parts, plus a motorcycle that looked like it was barely holding together.

"Do you want to go for a ride?" he asked. Bravely, I said "Okay," thinking he would just cruise around the block at 10 miles per hour.

He got me settled nicely on the back of his motorcycle, then took off like the winds of hell, until we hit the 401 . . . then he really opened it up. As we were going under an underpass, he pointed to a splash of red paint overhead. "That's the last guy who rode with me," he said with a grin. I guess I forgot to take my good humor pills because it was nowhere to be found in this tornado. We took a very long ride . . . too long! I was relieved to return home, crystalized in fright, as I fell off the bike. Brother Gregory laughed right from his belly button, at my frosty complexion. I think he could smell something I left on the seat as well, or perhaps in my pants.

The visit was wonderful, but short. We had to leave for Niagara Falls. In December, it's not the nicest place on the planet, but it was interesting and beautiful when they turned on the colored lights at night.

Our honeymoon was one month long, and we returned home with two large pieces of luggage, full of dirty clothes. What a nice introduction to married life! Willie had twenty dirty white dress shirts for me to wash and iron. I had never ironed a white shirt before, but tackled the job with a willing heart. Mother did all the ironing in our home, while I chopped the wood and carried in water and coal and tended to other outside chores. I was the man of the house. Domestic duties were totally foreign to me, but I was willing and determined to learn. Married life ran smoothly until Willie came to wear one of the ironed shirts. He was not impressed. "You didn't starch them!" he said in dismay. "I can't wear them like that!"

Slightly stressed out, I called my mother for advice on how to make starch. No problem. I cooked up a big batch, because I had twenty shirts to do. I starched them all . . . every square inch of them. Mother told me to sprinkle and roll them and it would make ironing easier. I followed her instructions, but ironing those starched shirts was something you would have to see to believe. When Willie came to wear his white shirt the following morning, he found twenty stiff white boards lined up in the closet. He was furious! I think he thought I did this to humiliate him. He couldn't fathom anyone being so stupid. In anger, Willie threw them all on the floor and kicked them across the room, then departed to drown his sorrows at the pub. It took me a whole day to iron those shirts and I was physically and emotionally exhausted.

Tearfully, I picked up the shirts that were scattered on the bedroom floor and called Perth's Laundry Service and had the shirts done professionally, for life. I vowed I'd never again iron another shirt for my 'understanding husband.' It was a promise I kept.

***

We rented an upstairs apartment in a home in the older part of town. It was fine for me. I wasn't accustomed to any degree of luxury. To have electricity and running water was more than I ever dreamed of.

One day, I was at home alone in this ancient two-story house that we now called home. It seemed to have a lot of strange creaky sounds coming out of its walls. I tried to ignore them, but today they seemed to be increasingly loud. I crept around the room in search of the noise location, and found it to be coming from downstairs. I stealthily tiptoed down the creaking staircase in my silky soft slippers, and noticed that the doorknob on the basement door was moving back and forth, like someone was trying to get in. There was a skeleton key in the lock and it was bobbing up and down, on the verge of falling out. Someone was trying to shake the key out of the lock. I panicked! I darted out the door, ran across the street and banged on a neighbor's door.

No one was home. I ran to the next house and did the same. A lady came to the door and I frantically told her someone was trying to break into our house. I stood shivering in the cold January wind, wearing just a light pair of pants and a cotton top that was designed for beach weather. She finally invited me in when the first icicle dripped off the end of my nose. She put her coat on and walked back home with me. *(What a brave lady.)* She walked inside and viewed the situation for a minute or two, then charged forth and opened the door. My heart was in my throat! I stepped back, ready to run for help. Out came a big black cat. Problem solved. I thanked the lady and crept upstairs like a deranged mouse.

We had been living in these rental quarters for a few nerve-wracking months when I found I was pregnant. Who expected that? Not me! I was never taught a thing about the birds and the bees. How many more surprises did life hold for me?

Pregnancy and I were not good friends. I was puking in the morning, puking in the evening, puking at supper time. That wasn't bad enough, I puked all over the bathroom floor, wall, and toilet at work. I tried to make it to the bowl, but I was a couple of feet shy when I upchucked. Jeanie, my co-worker, saw I was in trouble and came to my aid to clean up the mess. With a wet paper towel, she wiped my face, my hands, and my clothes. She guided me to a chair and said, "You sit here and calm yourself down. I'm cleaning this up, and no one needs to know it happened." What a sweetheart she was. I couldn't thank her enough, and I shall never forget her.

Morning sickness was a regular visitor. I simply had to quit work. I puked every morning for three solid months and Willie was not impressed. If he found me embracing the toilet bowl, he quickly left for work and didn't come home till late, and always drunk. This was an emotionally stressful time for me. I needed a kind word, an understanding hug, or a loving arm around me, which I didn't get. I cried a lot, and felt lost and alone in a strange unforgiving world I didn't understand.

Of course, everyone fully expected me to have a baby in eight months, otherwise, why would Willie be in such a hurry to marry a poor country bumpkin like me.

Willie's generous parents purchased a house for us. I'm not sure how this all formulated, but I do know I wasn't consulted. We had a mortgage that was more than two week's wages. Willie complained to his father and got a much-deserved raise in pay. The house was new and looked wonderful to me but it was cold and cost a fortune to heat. I had to wear a heavy jacket and rubber boots when doing the laundry in the basement. Water taps were on the opposite basement wall from the electrical outlet. This was totally inconvenient. I had a wringer washer but just an ordinary wash tub to do the rinse. I carried the tub across the room to the washer. I couldn't lift it with too much water in it, so I filled it up by carrying a small amount of water at a time. This wasn't the greatest arrangement, but a lot better than my mother had, so I didn't complain and just counted my blessings.

Willie was up north at the fish camp when it was time for me to give birth, eleven months, and seven days after our marriage. That must have knocked the socks off all predictions. I was visiting my parents when Mother recognized the birthing signs, and put me in a cab to go to my mother-in-law's place, which was closer to the hospital. They were out of town and my sixteen- year-old-brother-in-law took charge. He went to the lady next door and between them they made the decision. It was time for me to go to the hospital. Two days later, I gave birth to a six pound, three-ounce baby boy. I proudly named him after his father.

Shortly after my baby was born, a nurse came to my room and threw a piece of cloth at me and said, "Put this on," then swiftly left the room. Okay, I opened it up to see what it was and couldn't make any sense of it. It was approximately six feet long and about a foot and a half wide. I was puzzled. I was supposed to put this on, and I didn't think I was supposed to make a turban out of it, so I wrapped it around my tummy. When the nurse came back she was angry and disgusted that I didn't know what it was for. It was supposed to go around my breasts. She wasn't gentle taking it off my flabby tummy and wrapping it around my shoulders and heavily swollen breasts. This extra work made her dislike me immediately. She came back with an enema for me. She was pumping liquid up my back door with a vengeance, and I became most uncomfortable. I asked her to please stop.

"Just a bit more," she replied.

"I can't hold it much longer. Honest! I can't hold it!" I pleaded.

"Oh, yes you can," she said as she pumped another gallon of liquid up my rear exposure.

Suddenly the overloaded tank exploded all over the nurse, the floor, and bedding.

"I told you to stop," I cried with embarrassment, "but you wouldn't listen."

"You get up and go to the shower," she yelled in a controlled undertone that only she and I could hear. I staggered to the bathroom shower in the adjoining room and flicked on the water and passed out. I sat on the drain with the warm water flowing over me. Soon there was another mess for 'Miss Bridget' to clean up, as water overflowed into the room. No doubt they threw a 'going away party' when I was dismissed from the hospital.

A breast infection was traveling throughout the hospital, and severe restrictions were put on visitors. Only the husband and the patient's mother were permitted to visit newborn babies. Willie was out of town at his fish camp, and my mother couldn't leave my very ill father, so there was no one to visit me. Willie's sister Joan decided I needed a visitor and came to the hospital, posed as my mother. They couldn't possibly believe she was my mother, as she was only five years older than me, but they couldn't prove she wasn't. She had all the answers and was allowed in. I was thrilled to see her and even called her Mom for added effects. It was our little secret. Ten days later, she arrived again, this time, to take me home with my bundle of joy.

***

My son was breast fed every 20 minutes around the clock, and my breasts were as big as balloons and painfully raw. They were full of water, and my poor baby wasn't getting sufficient nourishment. I was doing my best, but it wasn't good enough, and Billy told me so. My doctor insisted that I breast feed and told me I wasn't trying hard enough. I wasn't getting any sleep and my little bundle of joy was not a happy camper. He had a good set of lungs that would have done wonders on a set of bagpipes. He was trying to tell me something was wrong, and I didn't understand. I was heading for a nervous breakdown, when my friend Beverly and her husband Mark dropped in to see the newborn baby. She saw the condition my child and I were in, and took charge. She had a house full of kids, so she knew what was wrong. "That child's hungry," she said. She sent her husband to the drugstore to purchase a baby's bottle, nipples, Karo syrup and Carnation milk. She sterilized the bottles and nipples and made a formula. Billy nearly swallowed the milk bottle and all, he was so hungry, then fell sound asleep and slept for six hours. I couldn't sleep because I thought he might have a convulsion from all that milk, but he woke up happy and smiling and asking for more. I didn't let the doctor know, but Billy was bottle fed from that day forward. On the Carnation milk, my son blossomed like a rose and became a beautiful little man, and I became a proud mother.

Willie managed to make it home to see his son when he was six weeks old. This was a good excuse to celebrate and drink . . . and the beat went on.

I said, "Willie, I wish you wouldn't drink so much. It's not good for you or our marriage. If you keep drinking like you have been, you could become addicted. You wouldn't want that, would you?"

He replied, "I have to drink. It makes me think better, work better, feel better, and I make better business deals when I drink with my customers. To stop drinking is out of the question. I wouldn't even want to quit. I enjoy it."

In tearful silence, I walked away. My baby was my comfort and my life.

Billy was two years old when he contacted the mumps. During the night, he became delirious and kept saying there were footprints walking on the ceiling in his bedroom. This frightened me out of my wits. I called the doctor, even though it was after midnight. He was understanding and kind and gave me instructions on how to bring the temperature down. I never left my baby's side until he completely recovered.

He no sooner got over the mumps when he got a terrible cold and cough. The doctor told me to steam the child. I didn't have a steamer, but I did have an electric kettle that produced steam. I promptly used it for the purpose. I was sitting on the side of my little boy's bed, watching his every move. I was terrified and exhausted, but angels were watching over us. The warmth and steam put me to sleep. I have no idea how long I slept, but I was suddenly awakened by a strange sound. Tick. Tick. Tick. Tick. I opened my eyes to see the kettle was dry and red hot. It was burning a hole in the hardwood floor. I quickly pulled the plug. It was only minutes, maybe seconds from bursting into flames. Willie was in the next room sleeping contentedly without a worry or a care. I was the mother, therefore the child and all issues connected to it, was my responsibility.

Billy survived the mumps, the flu, the measles, and all the childhood diseases and kept on growing like a weed, only much more beautiful.

Two years flew by and I became pregnant again.

Willie was drinking up a storm, and causing me no end of heartaches. He came home liquored up twenty out of thirty days a month. He stunk of liquor and his eyes looked strangely out of focus and totally spaced out. It made me nervous just looking at him. He would sit down to eat his meal and played with the food, giving one mouthful to the dog and the next mouthful to himself. When the plate was empty he would stagger off to bed. Next, he started bringing friends home at all hours of the night, and ordering me to cook them steaks, and entertain them by singing and playing the guitar. Sometimes he would abruptly exit the room and go to bed, leaving me with obnoxious strangers, and I would be obliged to gently ask them to leave. Often, they were reluctant to go because there was still rye in their glasses, and some left in the bottle. I solved the problem for them, and poured it down the sink. They took the hint and left, a little disgruntled. As they were leaving, one fellow said, "I'm going to tell Willie what you just did." I replied, "Not before I do," and slammed the door and locked it.

Willie started bringing one of my bridesmaid's home for supper. She didn't work close to his office, so arrangements to be picked up was the only way they could possibly meet. He said she wanted to see me . . . like he was doing me a favor, but they held hands under the table all the time I was preparing supper for them. I was supposed to be too stupid to notice. Well, I was stupid! I should have confronted them both instead of swallowing my pride.

Life went from bad to worse. Willie would phone to tell me he would be home for supper in twenty minutes. Four hours later he'd show up and dinner would look like a dog's breakfast by then, and he'd complain about my cooking. I got a bit huffed about his inconsiderate attitude and behavior, so the next time he phoned and said he would be home in 20 minutes, I waited for 25 minutes, to give him the benefit of the doubt, then I put the dinner in the freezer. He obviously wanted a cold dinner, and I aimed to please.

When he arrived home, and found he had a frozen dinner, he was furious. "I'll make my own damn dinner," he shouted. Staggering to the fridge, he opened the door and reached for an egg. It slipped from his fingers and smashed on the kitchen floor. He stamped his feet in anger and let out a few colorful curse words, then reached for another egg. It somehow went in the same direction as the first one. This made him totally upset. Swearing at the eggs he dropped, he grabbed another one and threw it on the floor.

"Oh, that's fun," I said, and I grabbed an egg and threw it on the floor too. He grabbed another one and I matched him one for one in this egg tossing tournament. I guess it was a tie because he went to bed hungry and I had the mess to clean up.

***

I was eight months pregnant and had been nowhere, done nothing but motherly duties since Billy was born, so I planned an outing to a movie with my mother and sister-in-law. I advised Willie that he was to babysit for me this one time. I took a taxi to the movie and enjoyed the evening immensely.

Traveling home, the taxi was broadsided by a car full of teenagers who had been drinking, and the taxi rolled over a couple of times, ending up in a Safeway parking lot. I saw what was coming and threw myself across the back seat and hung on. I was badly shaken and had a cut on my forehead, but that was all. The police came and recorded the accident in detail then drove me home. Of course, this took time. Willie was livid that I was out so late and decided to lock me out as a punishment. I banged on the door much longer than should have been necessary, then went to the bedroom window and banged and called. I got no response. I knew he could hear me and was just being a jerk, so I took a 2'x 4' from the garage and fired it through the window in the front door. That allowed me to reach inside and unlock the door. This action caught Willie's attention and he came running to open the door for me. He didn't say a word, but he had a startled look on his face. He obviously didn't expect that kind of action from me. We both settled down for the remainder of the night. We walked over the glass for three days before I finally gave in and cleaned it up.

The morning after the accident, at 8:00 a.m., the insurance agent was at my door to have me sign a release form. I signed that I was okay, not realizing I could have had a miscarriage because of this incident, but no one cared to advise me differently. Willie didn't even know I was in an accident. He didn't ask why I was late and I thought he wouldn't be interested in my story, so I didn't tell him.

***

Once again, Willie came home drunk, but this time he was feeling sick. He staggered into the bedroom and called to me to bring him a pail to puke in.

"You are capable of walking to the bathroom. Get in there if you are going to be sick," I said in disgust.

"I can't! I can't! Get me a pail. I'm going to be sick," he kept pleading like a child.

I had no patience for this sort of behavior and refused to oblige him with pail puking privileges, so he puked on the bedroom hardwood floor. I closed the door and left him to sleep with the stench. I crawled into bed with my little boy. Early next morning Willie rolled out of bed and stepped in his vomit. He did a fancy dance, then cursed and swore. "Get in here and clean up this mess, right now," he yelled in anger.

"Sorry, old boy," I said with emphasis, "I'm not cleaning up your drunken vomit."

"You are my wife, and it's your duty," he yelled. "My mother did this for Dad and me and so should you," he blubbered pathetically.

"Then I suggest you call your mother and have her come over and clean up this mess," I replied in a gentle tone.

Willie got dressed and stormed out the door without breakfast or even a cup of coffee. A couple of hours later his mother arrived with scrub pail in hand to do the cleaning, and I let her.

She said, "You know Deary, sometimes we have to do things in life we don't like to do."

I said, "You are absolutely right, but this isn't one of them."

***

Evangeline and Danny were our closest friends and we spent a lot of good times together. One night a group of our mutual friends decided we should all go dancing at the local Country Barn Dance Hall. Liquor was not allowed in public places in Manitoba at the time, so the menfolk tucked a 'mickey' in their coat pockets to smuggle indoors. They poured the liquor into their water glasses and were happily drinking, joking, and laughing, when the authorities walked in. Because our table was the noisy one, it was the one they chose to investigate. Each man was ordered to open his coat and reveal the contents of his pockets. Each lady had to open her purse to prove there wasn't anything illegal therein. I was the only person not guilty. The police were kind and considerate. They confiscated all the liquor and said if one person took the blame for the group it would be a much smaller fine. Willie didn't want his reputation tarnished, so he urged Danny to pick up the tab, but we all chipped in to cover the cost. That put a damper on the evening and we decided to leave and go to our house to finish the evening. As usual, Willie had a good supply of booze at home and willingly shared it with our friends. We played cards for twenty-five cents a game and it was a lot of fun. As the evening wore on the gang got tipsy, so at 4:00 a.m. I made strong coffee, sandwiches, and a variety of goodies to help sober them up for their drive home.

The next morning Willie was up at 6:00 a.m., feeling no pain. He was still inebriated from the night before, but insisted on visiting Evangeline and Danny to see what condition they were in.

Our friends lived on the outskirts of the city where they still used out-houses. When we drove in the yard, we noticed Danny working out back and Willie went to see what he was doing. Danny had moved the outhouse to one side, and with hip waders and a long-handled sieve he was searching for something. He felt sick when he got home from our house last night and headed for the outhouse where he threw up, and his teeth went flying down the hole. He wasn't flush with money and couldn't afford a new set of dentures. He had no choice, he had to find them. Scoop and sift, scoop, and sift. It wasn't a pleasant job, but with Willie heckling and laughing at him it was unbearable. He took a scoop of poop and fired it at Willie who managed to dodge the attack.

Danny eventually found his dentures and Evangeline scrubbed, cleaned, brushed, disinfected, and even boiled the false teeth in several batches of water, but even so, if you asked Danny a year later how his teeth were doing, he would gag. So much for drunken friends.

***

After my accident in the taxi, Mother Martha was concerned about me living alone with Billy, and had us come to stay with her for a time. It was always nice to go home to the peaceful, humble dwelling, where I always fit in. Billy was delighted to visit his grandpa and insisted on sleeping with him at night. Mother Martha tucked me in my old bed and I drifted off to dreamland. Morning came and I lay contentedly with my eyes closed, thinking of the chill of the day, and how Mother always got up early to start the fires so the family would have total comfort when they arose. She was such an angel.

Suddenly I felt something run across the blanket that covered my bulging belly. I let out a startled scream, as a rat vanished from sight.

Mother Martha came running to my side. "What is the matter my dear? Are you having pains?" she asked with concern.

"No, Mother, a rat ran over me! I saw him! He did, he ran right over my blankets!" I cried hysterically.

Daddy David and Billy showed up immediately. "I guess our three cats aren't working these days," Daddy said. "I will report this to the health department. This is where I draw the line! We are overrun with these rodents and no one is doing a thing about it. You can't stay here any longer, Jessie, if rats are taking over the household. Billy can stay here with us but I'll see you get back home today."

All the lots in the district where my parents lived were surveyed in two-acre narrow strips of land. Most owners cleared the back half for a vegetable garden and landscaped the front half for an attractive flower garden, home, and yard. The next-door neighbor wanted more privacy and built his home near the highway. He cleared very little of his property, leaving it mostly in the wild. The middle-aged owners of the land were running a small business operation on their premises. They cut strips of chamois *(which is the soft skin of sheep, deer, or goats)* for the lining of fur coats. These strips were wider at the top and slightly smaller at the bottom. Because of the shape, there were scraps of chamois to discard. The neighbor simply dumped the scraps in a pile out back in the bushes. Over fifteen or twenty years, the pile became a nice warm home for rats to occupy and breed. All the surrounding neighbors complained of seeing rats but our three cats seemed to be keeping them at bay, at least till now.

Daddy David busied himself making rat traps and selling them to neighbors. Once a rat was captured he had the means of connecting the trap to the exhaust of the car and asphyxiating the animal humanely. However, to have one run over his precious daughter, in her condition, caused him much concern. He planned to have the health department attend to this immediately.

Within a day, health inspectors arrived on the scene and ordered the neighbor to burn the pile of chamois, which they did. The rats made a hasty escape and spread out over the countryside for miles. Now the contained problem was a major one that kept the health department busy for years.

I packed my few possessions and headed back to the city, as my parents suggested. That night labor pains started and I phoned my sister-in-law Joan, who lived four short blocks away and she arrived within minutes to take me to the hospital. We were both pregnant and the admitting clerk looked us over rather strangely before asking the tender question, "Which one of you ladies is being admitted right now?" We had a good laugh and tension was released.

This birthing was normal and I was presented with a bundle of joy with black hair that stood up straight like porcupine quills. Her big sparkling eyes seemed to be delighted with her new environment. She weighed eight pounds, three ounces, and was pink as a rose petal. Her black hair was soon replaced with blonde hair the color of a sandy beach in midsummer sunshine. I knew she would be beautiful, that's why I called her Sandy. She was a perfect, healthy, happy, bottle fed baby, and she slept through the night. Often when I was spending my nights alone I would hold her in my arms, instead of putting her in her crib. She would watch TV with me and never complain. You'd almost think she understood what was happening on the screen. Billy played hard all day and slept all night, sometimes falling asleep at the supper table. It was lonely without Willie but my world was filled with the love of my children. They were so perfect, but deep down in my heart I knew my marriage wasn't.

I was concerned about getting pregnant again. I knew Willie would be all for it, but with his habitual drinking, I felt it was not a fit environment to bring in more children. I visited my doctor and asked for birth control. Doctor Zabbinski was very nasty and told me I had no right to use birth control, that it was a wife's duty to have children. I broke down crying in his office and between sobs I told him my husband was a drunk and I didn't want him to father more children.

The doctor sat in deep thought for several moments watching me cry my heart out, then said, "You have a son and a daughter, so I will allow you to have birth control. If you didn't have one of each, I wouldn't consider it." He wrote out the prescription and flung it at me as though I was dirt, then abruptly left the room.

Confused, ashamed, and feeling I had no human rights or control of my life, I left the doctor's office with determination, and found a drug store.

***

Our daughter was five months old and Billy was almost two and a half when Willie decided he would take his family with him to the fish camp on Lake Winnipeg. We left Battleship Bay around midnight on the evening of May 24, 1956. My husband and I, with our son and daughter, boarded the freighter called 'Lady Leeside' and set sail for Seagull Landing, located near the mouth of the Nelson River. It was a beautiful spring day, sunny and unusually warm for this time of year. I had never been far from home in my young life and found this adventure exciting and interesting. I was told we would be camping at the fishing station on Seagull Landing until August 1st /15th, depending on the weather. I had no idea what surprises awaited me.

Lady Leeside carried supplies to northern campsites, picking up the fisherman's catches, mainly pickerel and white fish, some jacks, perch, and sturgeon, for the return trip to the wholesale market. This freighter had a wooden hull and weighed 388 ton. It zipped along at the speed of eleven miles per hour, often carrying a cargo of 100 to 120 ton. It took a staff of seven, including the cook, to successfully navigate this freighter up and down the Red River, across Lake Winnipeg, up the Nelson River, to the fishing camp. Only the crew, hired fishermen and their families were lawfully allowed to be passengers on this licensed freighter.

The children and I were made as comfortable as possible in our tiny bunk. We snuggled down and peacefully slept to the gentle swaying of the ship.

When the morning sun peeked over the horizon, Billy, Sandy, and I were on the upper deck to greet the day. We enjoyed the sun and warm winds caressing our faces. By now we were well on our way to our destination and the only visible thing was sky and water. At times, they blended together in shades of translucent blue. I was discovering a fascinating new world.

Hearty meals were served on the boat and it was like a vacation to an exotic island, but the atmosphere was soon to change. By May 25th we were surrounded by ice. Slowly the boat navigated through the threatening ice floes. The farther north we traveled the larger the blocks of ice became. Most of them were approximately four to eight feet in diameter, blanketing around us as far as the eye could see. The thought of being marooned in the middle of nowhere till summer temperatures melted the ice away, was a concern weighing heavily on my mind.

Captain Conrad was highly experienced, and we had faith in his ability to navigate safely through these treacherous waters. He maneuvered the boat back and forth amid the ice floes until he found an opening and sailed fearlessly onward. It was a challenge for this capable, good- nature gentleman, and by May 26th we arrived safely at our destination. It wasn't quite the 'resort' I expected it to be.

The fish camp had a total of eleven permanent residents, but the fishing season increased the population to approximately 600.

As the boat pulled into dock, all I could see was a rugged looking cook shack, a matching ice house, a fish shed, and five tiny wooden bunkhouses. Between our camp site and our nearest neighbor, I counted 250 tents. There was no hotel. I could see no available living quarters for me and my family. I was stunned! I didn't know what to expect.

"You and the kids will wait on board the ship until we build living quarters for us," Willie stated matter-of-fact.

Shocked and somewhat bewildered, we headed back to our little cubicle to await the construction of our summer home, which I fully expected to be several days. Within 12 hours, four unprofessional carpenters built a 12' x 20' lean-to on the store. It was erected, complete with roofing, floor, small window, and homemade door. Beds were brought in from the ship and set in place. I brought bedding from home, so we moved in for the night . . . so did the mosquitoes. The roof rested on 2"x 4" studs and light could be seen around the top of the walls where it wasn't cased in. It was a convenient passageway for hungry mosquitoes, flies, moths, and fish flies. The children were bitten unmercifully. The only thing I could do to solve this problem was stuff paper in the openings at the top of the walls. I managed to find enough old newspapers and packaging material and scrunched then up, solidly stuffing the open areas and blocking out the bloodthirsty insects.

After oiling the children with mosquito repellent, they were tucked into bed with mosquito netting over them, and I soon followed. We were tired and slept well. The next day would be a busy one for everyone.

***

My assignment was to look after the store and keep a log of the fish our employed fishermen caught.

The crew got their daily needs in our store right after 6:00 a.m. breakfast. (The first breakfast was at 3:00 a.m.)

Willie helped me stock the store shelves with supplies and I was proud of my new responsibilities.

"You must never sell vanilla to anyone," he warned. "Some people will drink it and get dangerously drunk." I understood what he was saying. I heard similar stories before, and after living with him for a few years, I now understood what drunk meant.

However, later that day, when Willie was attending to the incoming fish, a handsome well-dressed young man with a generous head of blonde curly hair, came in and flashed his big blue eyes at me, and with a pleasant voice asked if he could 'borrow' a case of vanilla for the neighboring camp. He said his cook forgot to order it for the season. I knew the camps helped each other, so I didn't think there was any harm in giving him a case.

A few hours later Willie came running into the store in a panic. He slammed the store door shut and locked it, then ran to the back door and bolted it tight. Rushing to our living quarters, he secured it as well as he could. Out of breath, he inquired, "Did you sell anyone vanilla today?"

"No," I answered innocently, "but the cook across the lake, borrowed a case."

"Well, they knew you were a stranger, and an easy mark. They tricked you! There are six drunken men staggering up the pathway. They will want more vanilla! We must remain quiet. Don't answer the door or even talk."

This was no easy task with two small children. They must have sensed the urgency because they were extremely quiet.

A few moments later, there came a BANG! BANG! BANG on the store door. They called and cursed, kicked, and banged again and again. Then they went to our lean-to door and tried it, kicked it, and cursed even louder. That was scary because the homemade door was not strongly built. They continued their vigil till the wee hours of the morning. I was terrified, and Willie wasn't exactly feeling secure either. He sat silently with a club in his hand . . . the only defense he had.

While we were in confinement, we missed dinner and the late 9:00 p.m. coffee break, but we had lots of candy and cookies in the store to feed the children. We heard no complaints from them.

Eventually the inebriated battalion curled up together on the doorstep of the store and slept the remainder of the night.

In the early hours of the morning Willie removed all the vanilla supply to one corner of the warehouse, which was connected to the store, and piled cases of canned goods all around it. He knew what to expect. The men would be back. At 6:00 a.m. he opened the store and the doorstep lodgers bounded in. They searched every inch of the premises but found nothing. They eventually took their heavy heads back to their own camp. We never saw them again.

Willie was upset that I was hoodwinked by a smooth-talking man. It was a life lesson never to be forgotten.

We locked the store and went to the cook shack for breakfast. Billy loved to go there to eat. He thought the cooks name was "Cookshack" and that's what he called him. Cookshack was good to Billy and Sandy and made special cookies for them. The food he prepared was excellent and we were well fed.

Most of the day it was quiet in the store because the fishermen were out on the lake, so I had time to clean and fuss with the children and when my daughter was sleeping I would turn to knitting to amuse myself. Billy was exploring the premises in his walker and seemed to be happy looking at the store shelves. He could walk, but he loved to use the walker, and called it his car. It also kept him off the floor. He was a good child, usually, but prolonged silence caught my attention. I suspected he may be into something. I was right. He found a case of eggs and was happily breaking them to see all the 'stuff run out'. He had about two dozen eggs broken by the time I came on the scene. Several eggs were smashed in his hair and running down his neck and clothes. Cleaning the floor wasn't a difficult chore because I simply shoveled sand from the beach on top of the messy eggs and scooped it up to discard. Cleaning Billy's hair and clothing took a little more time and patience. I didn't tell the boss about this event. I chalked it down to a 'breakage' write-off.

Billy wanted to play in the sand in front of the store. That seemed to be a safe enough area for him to play, and it was well within my sight, but he found a nice little round stone and pushed it up his nose. It started to hurt and he began to scream. I ran to rescue him. When I saw the problem, I panicked! I knew the nearest hospital was Hudson House, 20 miles away, by boat. I left my daughter in her stroller, picked up my son and ran with him to the dock where Willie was filleting fish. Being of a calmer nature than I, he successfully retrieved the stone. This disaster aged me ten years in ten seconds. Upon returning to the store, which was about 200 yards away, I found the till had been emptied. Sandy was fine and the catastrophe successfully taken care of, so I didn't worry about the missing money.

***

Lice were prevalent in the community, and it was a chore to keep them away from the children. The village children were attracted to my little blonde offspring and wanted to play with them. It was heart wrenching having to keep them apart, but I had little choice. Families would enter the store carrying the 'beasts' and my only defense was to keep the children isolated. It wasn't uncommon to see families searching each other for lice, and when they captured them they cracked them with their teeth . . . which absolutely nauseated me! Every single day, I disinfected the store and everything in sight. I washed the counters and wooden floors with sixty percent lake water, twenty percent Javex and twenty percent Pine Sol. The disinfectant was at least a clean smell.

***

Fish were cleaned at the water's edge, and the guts were dumped in the same spot. Our water supply was taken from the same body of water, only a few feet past the end of the dock where they considered the water to be much cleaner. I chlorinated the water for my family but other members of the community refused my offer to purify their water supply, until dysentery broke out, then they flocked to my door for help. I put them on boiled water and sugar until the problem subsided. I had a supply of Kaeopectate which I shared with them, and for this service I earned the name of "Nurse", which I am not.

I had to skim fish flies off the top of our drinking water before boiling it, but it still tasted and smelled of fish. They were everywhere. They were so thick they made a blanket covering the ground that scrunched beneath our feet as we walked through them. They coated tree trunks like fur jackets. Our laundry smelled fishy and no matter how much I boiled, scrubbed, or bleached, the pungent odor permeated the washing. Everyone simply learned to live with it.

The night watchman was the best in the world. He patrolled the camp at night in his scrubby looking work clothes and miner's boots, carrying a big club for protection. He also used the club for wake up calls. He pounded on all the tents and bunkhouse doors every morning at 3:00 a.m. announcing the break of day. He entered our living quarters cautiously, singing 'tie dee dee, tie dee dee,' to announce his intrusion, and would stoke up the fire so we would have a warm room for the start of our day. He carried water in and placed it on the heater for our daily scrub down, and filled the wash tubs for me on wash day. It took almost a day to heat water to do laundry. Scrubbing on the washboard wasn't new to me. I did my best with what I had to work with.

***

The Lady Leeside freighter arrived every third or fourth day, depending on the weather, to pick up the freshly ice packed fish to transport to Winnipeg markets. There was a large building that held 1500 tons of ice, which was prepared over the winter by the local inhabitants. When it was needed in the fish sheds, a shore hand used a pick axe to grip the blocks of ice and heave them down a slide to where the fish were being packed for shipping. One day in mid-season, a shore hand swung his pick axe a little too hard and it slipped out of his hand. It landed on the instep of a worker below. The employee had a pair of miner boots on, but the axe went right through and pierced his foot, about a half inch deep. He was writhing in pain. Fellow workmen carried him to the store for me to 'do something.' I was twenty-three years old, with no First Aid training, but I knew he needed immediate attention, so I did my best. The man was in shock! I remembered hearing my mother tell stories of by gone days, about an accident that required her immediate attention or the victim would bleed to death. The method she used came to mind. Several men assisted me in removing the workman's miner boot. This was quite a struggle and caused a great deal of pain to the accident victim. I think we all felt the pain this poor man was going through. I prepared warm water and poured in a half box of salt. I had the patient soak his foot to clean it as much as possible. Then I poured a full bottle of mercurochrome on the wound. It bled profusely! I knew he would bleed to death before he reached the hospital, which was a two-hour boat trip to Hudson House. I took a loaf of white bread and cut it in half lengthwise and placed one half over the wound and tied it in place with a towel. I made a tourniquet with one of my scarves and instructed the men to release it every five to ten minutes. I didn't know exactly how often it should be released, but I knew it must be done. We packed ice around the leg and the co-workers carried the patient to an available motorboat. It pulled away at top speed, and I broke down crying. I was totally shaken from this experience and breathed a prayer for this poor fellow's safety.

At the Hudson House hospital, the doctor asked who had done the preparation. He said, "It may be an old wives remedy, but she saved your life."

***

The only communication with the outside world, at these fishing stations, was a two-way radio. Willie called home each morning, weather permitting. It was a time we gathered around to hear gossip from other camps and news from home.

The entertainment center at our station was a small log church that Reverend Fairweather built from logs he personally cut and hued by hand. He made some wooden benches and a little steeple with a bell that rang out the invitation to attend his services. He made everything by hand and it was a work of art. He held services in this pretty little church every Sunday and a few locals attended along with my two children and myself. Upon completion of the church, the United Church of Canada transferred him to another location. He was heartbroken. I felt sorry for him, as I witnessed the labor of love that went into the construction of this tiny place of worship.

***

The fishing season was over and we sailed home uneventfully - August 15, 1956.

Back home, Willie purchased a new 1956 Pontiac car and was excited to show it off. He invited the children and me to go for a ride. He drove around for 20 or 30 minutes and passed a pub that was one of his hangouts. He stopped the car abruptly in front of the Lockport Hotel, then said, "I have to go in here for a minute, I won't be long." I thought he wanted to show some of his cronies his new vehicle, so I didn't say anything.

It was a hot, humid day, and clouds of mosquitoes were out in full force. This made it extremely uncomfortable because we couldn't open the windows. We were sweltering in the summer sun that was beating through the car windows. We suffered for three quarters of an hour and I couldn't stand it any longer. Billy and Sandy were crying and being eaten alive by mosquitoes. I told the sobbing children to sit tight, that mommy was going to get daddy, and I ran quickly into the pub. A guard was at the door. He raised both hands boldly before my face and announced with authority, "Sorry madam, Manitoba law doesn't allow ladies in a pub."

"That's okay Sir," I replied, "Right now, I'm not a lady. I'm a very angry wife and mother," and I barged past him, and into the pub. I saw Willie seated around a large table with a group of men, laughing and drinking. I walked over to him and grabbed a handful of his blonde curly hair and dragged him out of the building. I could hear roars of laughter, clapping, whistling, and hooting, but I didn't care. I got Willie, and we drove home in silence. For the rest of the week Willy kept his constitution well lubricated as he celebrated the ownership of his new car and the freedom of being home for a short time.

***

Noon, August twenty-fifth, we set sail once again, this time we were heading north to Majestic Point. We entered Lake Winnipeg from the Red River and were sailing along at top speed when the first mate went off range, and the Lady Leeside hit a sand bar. The heavily loaded freighter tipped to the port side, 30 to 45 degrees. Life boats were lowered and some of the cargo was unloaded onto an inspector's boat that happened to be in the general proximity at the time. This allowed the freighter to rise in the water so the inspector's boat could tow us off the sandbar, and we could continue our journey.

Meanwhile, I was sitting on deck with the two children. The bench we were sitting on began to slide toward the water. I wrapped my arms around my babies and braced my foot against a railing to secure us until help came. Everyone was concerned about the boat problem and didn't notice that the children and I were in trouble. It seemed about a half hour before Willie came to rescue us. We were taken on board the inspector's boat until the problem was righted.

The rest of our trip was pleasant. Weather cooperated, and we arrived at Majestic Point on August twenty-sixth for the beginning of the fall fishing season. I was happy to have my friend Evangeline along on this venture, to keep me company.

The day after we arrived at the fishing station, the cook and the cookie quit. This was a major disaster as Willie had fifty fishermen to feed. There was no alternative, Evangeline and I became instant camp cooks. I must admit my friend knew more about cooking than I did, and even made homemade bread for the hungry fishermen. I was on the potato detail and peeled, with a paring knife, forty to fifty pounds for each dinner and supper meal. The men worked hard and had healthy appetites. We had no cook books to guide us, but we did our best and came up with some great concoctions. No one complained.

We were up at 4:00 a.m. every morning, providing bacon and eggs, pancakes, toast, and coffee for the 6:00 a.m. breakfast. By 10:00 a.m. we were expected to provide coffee with pie, biscuits, cookies, cake, etc. Lunch was a full course meal and 3:00 p.m. was coffee and goodies again. The evening full course meal was 6:00 p.m. and all leftovers of the day were served at 9:00 p.m. coffee break. Every scrap of food was cleaned up at the end of each day. There were no leftovers to worry about. They ate until every morsel vanished. It was a long day but the men were kind to us and didn't complain about the quality of food, so long as there was plenty of it.

It was near the end of the fishing season when Willie realized he was over-stocked with canned Klik and pork and beans, so he canceled all orders of fresh meat. For two long weeks, we served Klik luncheon meat in the most creative ways. We fried, baked, cubed it in sauces, sliced it cold, cubed and mixed it with beans as hash, wrapped it in pancakes etc. Each meal was a challenge. We opened thirty to forty cans of both Klik and beans for each meal. As I was opening these cans, my fingers and wrists began to ache and pain from the strain of constantly turning the old fashioned can opener. I started to sing to distract myself from the discomfort. The job had to be done. I sang:

"Beans and Klik, beans and Klik, ain't it enough to make you sick?

But when you get tired, we change the scene, from beans and Klik, to Klik and beans."

It helped keep the morale up, and brought a smile to the faces of the unfortunates who had to eat it. Somehow, we managed to make it through the season.

Family life was close to perfect. There were no luxuries but we were together as a family and Willie didn't have any liquor to drink. Who could ask for more?

***

November 1, 1956, we anxiously watched the horizon for the freighter to appear. It was a long two months since we left home, and I was especially anxious to leave Majestic Point, which is located approximately at the western midsection of Lake Winnipeg. In winter, the population is three, but it becomes a bustling village of approximately 200 during fishing season. Evangeline and I were the only Caucasian women in this lonely part of the world, 150 miles from home, by water.

Not only was the fishing season over, but winter had settled in. Three feet of snow covered the ground and cold cutting winds off the lake chilled you to the bone. I was straining my eyes to spot a tiny dot of hope on the horizon, an indication that the boat was coming to take us home. All I could see was white frothing waves snapping at an angry dark sky. Everyone seemed confident that the boat would eventually come for us, but my faith was failing me.

Daily activities continued as the fishermen eagerly prepared for the return trip. It was a successful season and everyone was anxious to see their families. I had a burning desire to get out of this place and was packed for days. It had been a trying experience . . . one I shall never forget. While I was working long hours with two little children under foot, Evangeline was seven months pregnant. We met our challenges head on, and supported each other cheerfully.

I longed for the comforts of home, but dreaded the return voyage. However, I was happy the season was over, and boarding the ship was the only way out of this God forsaken hole. I kept a concerned lookout for the freighter on the horizon. The snow kept falling and I feared the lake would freeze over, although I kept this thought to myself.

Excited voices told me the long-awaited vessel was spotted. My heart pounded in rhythm with the splashing waves slapping the shore. I watched the advancing ship valiantly fighting stormy conditions until she pulled into dock. Spirits were high as everyone piled on board – men, women, and children, with our meager belongings. By midnight we set sail. Even before leaving the dock, I thought we were destined for a terrifying trip. I was right. The tossing became more ferocious as the night progressed.

My children and I were given privileged quarters on the upper deck. We were provided with bunk beds that were adorned with well used mattresses, in a tiny compartment that provided just enough room to stand to dress. Our suitcases with essentials were placed on the top bunk where I was supposed to sleep. The children were nestled together on the bottom bunk. Thankfully, I had my own blankets to cuddle into. The crudely made door had a simple latch hook to shut out the weather. We had no heat, and a tiny window above the top bunk allowed a small amount of light to filter in. I had a homemade toilet box . . . a hole cut in a wooden butter box and a pee pot placed underneath. It was an essential piece of equipment, as it was impossible to take the children below deck during a storm. I snuggled in with the children to give them comfort and warmth, and we settled in for the journey home.

I peered out the window into solid darkness and wondered how the captain knew where he was going. At first the ship rolled to the starboard. It seemed to reach forty-five degrees and halt, for what seemed an eternity. I held my breath! Fear was restricting my breathing. There were times when I was sure the boat was not going to right itself . . . we were going to sink. I knelt beside my precious children and cupped them in my arms. Their warm bodies gave me strength to hold on. I had to, I had to save my babies. We were at the mercy of the wind and waves. The boat creaked and shifted to the port side, again to forty-five degrees and halted. Once again fear overwhelmed me. "Dear God," I prayed. "Have mercy on us and calm the waves. Please take us home safely." All night we rolled from side to side as the captain struggled to maintain control.

The children became seasick and vomited all over the blankets. I had no change of bedding and no water to clean them up. I used shirts, underwear, socks and whatever I could find to wipe up the puke, and tossed the items overboard. I put the children at the opposite end of the bed where it was dry. There are no words to adequately describe the stench in the cubicle we were imprisoned in, with no possible means of escape. Throughout the night my babies took turns vomiting. I was seasick as well, but I had to function through it. I tried to sing to the children and tell them stories, but they felt the surging and heaving of the boat and sensed the terror in my voice and clung to me desperately.

After what seemed an eternity, morning came. It was November 2. We must have changed direction, as the ship was now heading into waves that were thirty feet high, I was told. I could see the water splashing past my miniature window. It was rough, but not as scary as when the boat rolled from side to side.

I heard the call for breakfast from the belly of the boat, but I wouldn't attempt taking two little children down the narrow metal stairs on the outside of the freighter. About an hour later Willie came to the door with a plate of toast. As he passed it to me, a wall of water nearly washed him away.

He grabbed the door for anchor, as the toast came flying inside. I was glad to have some food for the children, but I couldn't eat a thing.

Willie returned to the kitchen where coffee and much stronger drink was readily available.

Up and down we tossed on Lake Winnipeg, 9,460 square miles of violently angry water. The children and I took turns vomiting until we had nothing left to bring up. I still retched and the pain made me double over. My knees were weak and shaky. My head was light and dizzy and my eyes had difficulty focusing. The odor in our confinement multiplied, with both children now suffering from diarrhea. The three of us were ill.

I had no means of washing diapers or my baby's tender buttocks. To my knowledge, disposable diapers had not yet been invented and with each changing I had to heave overboard whatever it was I was using for a diaper. I used towels, shirts, underwear, blouses or whatever I could find to substitute. Soon their little bottoms were painfully red and raw. This discomfort made them cranky, miserable, and demanding of attention. The only thing that kept me from jumping overboard was the love I had for my children. I had a burning desire to save their lives at all cost.

In good weather, it would normally take 18 hours to travel from Majestic Point to Winnipeg. We had been traveling 24 hours and still no land in sight. My portable toilet, which we were using out of desperation and necessity, was brimming. It had to be emptied. I steadied myself as best I could and opened the door to pour the contents overboard. At that precise moment, a huge wave came splashing over the boat, knocking the door back. The pee pot was thrown back at me. I was drenched in urine from head to toe. I gagged and retched and gagged again! "If there's a hell, then I'm in it right now," I cried out in horror. I found a change of clothing, and without the luxury of a bath or even a superficial wash, I cleaned myself up the best I could.

On we sailed into the night. By midnight, the sound of excited voices could be heard. We must be near land. Home! What a heavenly thought! The tossing subsided . . . then I felt the bump. Yes, we had reached land! Thank God! I waited patiently for my orders.

Finally, Willie came to the door and said, "We've landed at Hogan's Island. We will spend the night here or until the storm clears. Get your things together and let's go," he shouted.

"Where will we stay," I meekly inquired. "Is there a hotel here?"

"No," Willie replied, "but I know some good people who will put us up for the night." He took Billy's hand and our suitcase, and I carried Sandy down the dark narrow stairway to the lower deck. They had placed a narrow plank from the boat to the dock and Willie took our son across safely. I took one look at the warped, rickety looking plank bobbing up and down with the waves, and I froze with fright. As desperate as I was to reach land, extreme terror prevented me from moving a single muscle. Never in my life had I ever felt such intense fear.

"Come on, Jessie! Get off!" Willie hollered. "What's the matter with you? Get over here!

I can't help you. I have Billy to take care of."

I was speechless and I couldn't move! I had no feelings.

One of the First Nation's deckhands noticed my distress and took my baby from my arms. I was expected to walk the plank alone, but I was frozen on the edge of an unknown universe. I had no feeling, other than fear. I was spaced out!

The deckhand passed Sandy to another member of the crew and came back to rescue me. Trembling, I reached out for his strong reassuring hand and ventured to take one step. I looked down between the boat and the dock and shrieked, "Oh, my God! There's a body down there! There's a dead body floating down there! My God, do something!" Tears were streaming down my face, and I was shaking violently, and screeching pathetically.

"Don't be so damned stupid," I was promptly told, as laughter rang out in the background. "We are too busy to play around with your stupid imagination! Now get over here, unless you want to spend the night on the boat." The thought of remaining on the boat a moment longer was enough to jolt me into action. I reached for the gentleman's hand and grasped it tightly and somehow managed to walk across the bouncing board. I was on land!

Willie took us to the home of Henry and Helen Townsend who lived year-round in this isolated village. They were kind and generous people and welcomed us in their humble home, even though our arrival was after the midnight hour. "Come in my dears. Come in," Helen said in a soft friendly voice. "You are welcome to stay here with us till the storm dies down. What can I get you folks? How can I help?"

"I'm embarrassed to ask, but would you happen to have any diapers?" I asked.

Helen laughed a jolly laugh and said, "It's been many years since I've had to use diapers. My children are grown up, but I'll see what I can do." She opened a huge cupboard door and took new flannelette sheets out. Without a thought of the cost, she tore them up to make a stack of diapers. She helped me bath and change the children, supplying Vaseline and corn starch for their raw little bottoms, fed them, and tucked them in bed. I found some clean clothes for me and I enjoyed a hot bath where I tried to scrub the experience of filth away from my body and mind. When I came out, Helen had lunch and a cup of strong coffee for me. It was the best coffee I had ever tasted. I was exhausted and conversation was difficult for me, so Helen tucked me in a comfortable cot, just like a loving mother would do, and I slept.

When morning came, the news of the storm was discouraging. "No way can we continue the journey home," said Willie. "We have to wait out the storm."

"Don't worry," said Helen, "You can stay here until the ill wind dies down," and she did everything she could to make us comfortable. "We have rescued many people in our lifetime," she said. "This is nothing new for us. We are happy to help."

I longed to see my parents. I knew they would be worried about my safety and the welfare of their grandchildren, but there was no way to contact them to let them know we were safely on land.

Later that morning, the sad news came. A man had been found in the waters between the boat and the dock. A local man had fallen in and drowned. He was well known for tipping a few too many pints of bubbly and probably came out to meet and greet our freighter. I felt dreadfully sad.

I saw him floating in the waters below me, but no one would listen. Was he still alive when I spotted him? Could his life have been saved if they had listened to me? Why didn't someone try? Why didn't someone care? Why? Why? Why? I was depressed for days because of this tragedy. I couldn't wash it out of my mind.

We stayed at the Townsend home for two more days and enjoyed their gracious hospitality. Nothing was too good for us, and we appreciated their friendship and generosity.

Finally, Willie came with the news we all wanted to hear. "Tomorrow morning, we will take a yawl across to the mainland. A car will meet us on the other side." That was music to my ears. We were going home at last.

It was a two mile stretch of shallow water that we must carefully navigate. We piled our luggage, high chair, walker, five adults and two children, into this twenty-foot boat. There was little room to spare. In favorable weather, a ferry traveled this route but today it was too rough, so the ferry captain offered to take us across in his yawl. We cheerfully accepted the offer.

"No one is to move during this entire trip," the captain informed us sternly. "If we shift the weight we will capsize. We are overloaded, so stay put, if you know what's good for you!"

I looked down and realized the unabridged truth he had spoken. The boat was floating three inches out of the water. "My goodness, this isn't safe!" I gasped. Then looking around at the silent passengers, I realized this was simply another desperate attempt to reach home. Everyone was solemnly motionless. We moved slowly, scraping bottom, and hitting rocks all the way. With each bump and scrape my heart skipped a beat. I wondered if this humble, overloaded yawl, could withstand the test. If we hit a big rock would it split the boat in half? Would it tip over and empty us, contents, and all, into the water? I was numb. There was no fear of me rocking the boat . . . I was so frightened I was barely breathing.

Somehow, by the grace of God, we made it across the shallow waters. We were safe at last. Home was a short 85 miles of highway driving ahead. Once I put my foot on dry land it stayed there permanently. I would never sail again.

***

My wages for running the camp kitchen was $300.00. I was thrilled. They didn't pay me for looking after the store and the books at the last camp, so it was a definite surprise. I knew immediately what I would spend it on, and it wouldn't be Klik. I would purchase a piano. I took my father with me to make sure I got a good one. He was a great musician in his younger days and was thrilled that I inherited the love of music. We chose a beautiful restored Bell piano with excellent tone quality, but it was $100.00 more than I had. Daddy David reached in his pocket and paid the difference. That was the first time he ever contributed to any of his children's musical training, and I was deeply touched.

Willie arrived home to see the piano in the living room. "Okay," he said, "Play, Home on the Range." After a fashion, I managed to pound out, with one finger, a sound he could identify. Now play, "You are my Sunshine," he happily requested. I couldn't do it and he was upset. "It's a pretty expensive toy if you can't play the darn thing," he muttered in disgust.

"I just fulfilled the promise you made to me before we got married. Perhaps you forgot, but I didn't," I replied with tears in my eyes. I guess I expected him to be as happy as I was with this wonderful purchase, but he wasn't.

My in-laws had plenty to say about my extravagance, but my heart was so thrilled with the instrument, I never heard a word they said. I knew someday I would play beautiful music and they would be proud of me.

***

Willie still made his three or four excursions a year to fishing camps, all over the Manitoba/Ontario regions. The only good thing I can say in favor of this is, he wasn't drinking most of the time when he was away from home. There were no pubs, beer parlors or liquor commissions in these undeveloped areas, and his luggage could only handle a small amount to be transported there. On the mainland, it was a constant twenty-six oz. heartache for me. There was always liquor available at the fish plant office in Winnipeg, and it was customary for the men to gather in the boss's office after work, and chat about the day's events and get soused. Never did Willie arrive home without his belly full of booze and a mouth full of razor blades. There was no point in fighting back . . . it was a losing battle, and I was always wrong, no matter what the subject of contention happened to be. He had to blame someone, and I became his convenient kicking board. I got to the point where I just took the abuse and remained quiet. Without feedback, he would eventually wind down, and stumble off to bed.

About this time, my dear old daddy, David McGann, passed away. It was a huge loss to me as Daddy had always been there for me. He was an ill man, but also a pillar of strength during my growing up years. He was raised a devout Methodist and passed his strict upbringing on to his family. Honesty was on the top of his list. I was fortunate to have both a mother and a father at home, guiding and protecting me from the wrath of the world, but I was never educated about the birds and the bees or the perils of gambling, or the almighty bottle, and how it could destroy a person and/or the world around them.

Mom and Dad had always idolized Willie. He was especially kind to both of my parents and managed to present a 'happy-go-lucky' sober image when in their company. He was a blessing to them in many ways, supplying them with fish and donating all the insulation for their new home free of charge, and many other things too numerous to mention. He would do anything for them. This made it difficult for me as I had no support system. I was on my own, and felt alone against the world.

Willie had a lot of good qualities. Everybody loves a happy drunk, and they loved him even more because he was so generous with his money, and his booze. Every Christmas he made sure all the families with children that he knew, got a case of oranges and apples, a bottle of whiskey and often twenty dollars for each small child. He was generous to a fault, but not always for the good of mankind. This loving the good in Willie and hating the rotten side of him made my life a painful up and down slippery slope, and as bumpy as my first toboggan ride.

I had two beautiful children in my life because of Willie. I loved them with all my heart and soul, and they were generous with their love for me. They loved their father unconditionally, especially when he was drunk and passed out twenty-dollar bills to them and their friends, to buy candy. Who wouldn't love a joker like that? I couldn't leave him because of the children.

They needed a home, an education, and security that I knew I couldn't provide. I loved them too much to deprive them of that. I didn't count anymore. My life was put on the back burner.

Just about the time I would be feeling 'this is the last straw' and I'm not going to be his doormat any longer, Willie would come bouncing in the house with a magnificent gift . . . like a mink jacket or a pearl and diamond studded dinner ring, or a new dress or sweater for me. Emotions were on a constant roller coaster ride. I knew he loved me in his own messed up way, and I loved the little boy Willie could be when he needed me. It was the other side of sober that was the killer.

Money came easy to Willie . . . at least it seemed that way because he threw it around carelessly, which accumulated a wide range of so-called friends. I have no idea how much he gambled during these years. He would never discuss finances with me. "That's the man's department," he would state with arrogance.

Early one Sunday morning there was a loud BANG, BANG, BANG, on the front door. I flew out of bed to answer the urgent call. I had just turned the key, and was about to open the door and it was pushed open in my face, and nearly knocked me over. A strange man, wearing an unfriendly face, demanded, "Where's Willie?"

In a trembling voice, I stammered, "He's in bed sleeping."

"Tell him to get the hell out here right now, before I come in and drag his sorry ass out, and tell him to bring the check book along for good luck."

Startled, terrified, and shaking in my pajamas, I ran to rouse Willie, to give him the urgent message. He scrambled into his pants and went out with his check book in his hand.

I sauntered by to see what was happening, and Willie was writing something in the check book. I noticed his hands were shaking. The angry visitor snatched the check, and took off down the steps to his car. He burned rubber as he pulled away.

Willie closed the door quietly and went back to bed without saying a word. He stayed there the whole day, and refused my offer of food. He gave no explanation, and I asked no questions.

I knew better than that.

I often found rolls of money under the bed, or on the seat of the unlocked car that had been parked on the street all night. I always gave him the money I found. Someone in this world had to be honest.

***

Willie's sense of humor was often badly warped when he was drinking. There were times when we were going somewhere in the car, and just for fun, Willie would go through red lights. He would announce ahead of time that he was going to do this, and I would freak out and plead with him not to do such a crazy stunt. He loved it when he made it through safely and all the cars screeched to a stop, missing him by inches. He would laugh hysterically. I'm convinced there's a group of guardian angels assigned to watch over drunks. I couldn't stand this any longer and quit driving in a car with him. It was inconvenient, but much safer.

Willie never wanted me to drive. It was just another controlling factor, but as the children started attending different activities it was becoming a necessity. The next time Willie was out of town, I took driving lessons. The lessons went well, and it was time for me to take my test and receive my license. We got in the lineup waiting for my turn, and the instructor went over details that could possibly cause me to fail, and he said, "Don't worry, just do your best. The biggest hurdle will probably be parallel parking."

"What's that?" I inquired.

The instructor looked at me in shock. "Oh, dear, I don't think I taught you that. Well, here's what you do." He gave me a three-minute lesson and I was called to take my test. I passed the driving part with flying colors. "Now let me see you parallel park," I was told. Calmly, I did exactly as my instructor said to do, and made a perfect park. My instructor was watching from across the street, and couldn't believe his eyes. I got my license that day but took a couple of parking lessons anyway, just for good luck.

When Willie came home, I showed him my accomplishment with pride. He was not impressed. I got lectured and lectured, over and over, on how women were not capable of driving. Disgusted with this turn of events, he left for his office. After a few hefty drinks of whiskey, he picked up the phone and called me. "Take a taxi to my office immediately. I need your help," he ordered. My intuition told me the warning sign was red, but I did as he requested. When I got to the fish plant he told me to drive one of his two-ton trucks home, as he would need it in the morning. I knew he was trying to prove a point, so I got in and drove it home. I drove slowly and often had to use two feet on the brakes to make it stop, but with determination and faith in my higher power, I parked the truck in front of our house. The next day he asked me to park his car behind the office building. It was hooked up to a boat and trailer. Don't ask me how I did it, but I did. I'm sure the car was angel powered. He didn't like it, but he had to accept the fact that I could drive. His lack of control called for a few more drinks with the boys.

Willie didn't have much choice, he bought me an old Studebaker car to transport the children around. It had no inside panels on the doors, and no heater, so he didn't have to worry about me leaving town in the winter months. The children and I wore snowsuits and flight boots, mitts, scarves, and toques because we had to drive with the windows open, or they would frost up in the cold winter temperatures. This didn't stop Billy's hockey player friends from piling in the back for a ride home. I enjoyed hearing their laughter and constant chatter, and I loved getting a hockey stick in my ear now and again.

Willie conceded, I was making good use of the old relic and upgraded my vehicle to a 1954 Buick. A few years later he purchased a new 1966 Pontiac Strata Chief for me as a Company asset. Now I was driving in high class and comfort. My mother-in-law was a silent partner in the family business, so that gave her the authority to use me as a taxi, to drive her around town to shop whenever the spirit moved her. Time was not my own, and often interfered with my projects . . . like painting the kitchen, baking, or washing clothes or cutting the grass. I'd drop everything to drive her, at her whim, to her favorite shopping center. I finally got my Irish up! Enough was enough! I presented the car keys to my husband, with thanks, but no thanks. "This car is not mine. I'm just a taxi, and an underpaid one at that. So, I hereby cancel my contract to transport your mother around town when she can well afford a taxi. If you want me to have a car to take the children to their activities, then put it in my name. I'll accept nothing less." My demands were met with a little reluctance.

It was close to Christmas, and I had a lot of shopping to do. I parked at the Mall and made my way through the crowds, while keeping one eye on my children. My shopping cart was full and it was time to head back home. Billy and Sandy jumped in the back seat of the car and I piled the parcels around them and put some on the front seat as well. I felt satisfied with my purchases and proceeded to start the car. It wouldn't start! There wasn't a sound of any kind coming from the motor. I was stunned and didn't know what to do for a second or two, then I locked the kids in the car, and went back in the store to call my husband for help.

"Willie, my car won't start. I'm stranded out here with the kids and my purchases, at the North End Mall," I informed him with much concern.

"Don't tell me your troubles. I'm in bed and I'm staying here. If the car won't start, call the garage man to fix it," he said, and hung up the phone.

Pete, the garage man we dealt with, lived in the south part of town. It was rather cold, and it was after 9:00 p.m. His working day was over. I hated asking him for help but didn't have any alternative. I explained my predicament and he was kind enough to travel all the way across town to rescue me, my children, and my mega Christmas parcels. I waited patiently for him to arrive, frosting up the windows all the while. Finally, he drove up and parked beside me and jumped out of his car with a grin a mile wide on his friendly face. "Jessie, my dear," he said with a chuckle, "do you know why your car won't start? This is not your car!"

"Oh yes, it has to be. I opened the door with this key and it goes in the ignition. It has to be mine."

"Look at the license plate, Sweetie. It's not yours." He was holding his sides with laughter. I got out of the car to look, and to my dismay, it was not my car. Mine was parked three cars over. Pete helped me move my children and all my packages to the right car, and made sure it started before waving me a happy good-bye.

What a great guy Pete was, to handle this goof-up with such charm. I'm so thankful the owner of the car I was trying to start, wasn't finished shopping yet. I would have had a lot of explaining to do. I'm sure they are wondering to this day, how the windows of their car got frosted up.

***

One night, Willie wanted to visit a relative on the other side of town, but I wouldn't go. I knew it would be another night of drinking, and I wanted no part of it. He invited my thirteen-year-old niece, who happened to be visiting us at the time, to accompany him, and off they went for the evening. I stayed home, doing chores, and taking care of our children. It was getting late and the kids were in bed sleeping, so I toddled off to do the same. About 1:00 a.m. I heard Willie arrive home. I just rolled over and continued with my much-needed rest. About 4:00 a.m. the phone rang. A man's voice asked if Willie Masterson was home. I was annoyed and shouted, "Yes, he is home, where all decent, respectable people should be at this hour of the night!"

"I'm sorry to disturb you," he said respectfully, "but this is the Winnipeg Police department calling. I'm afraid someone has stolen your car. We found it in a ditch full of water on the outskirts of the city."

"Hold on" I said, as I ran to get Willie. "Come quickly! Someone has stolen your car," I said as I shook his inebriated body. "The police are on the phone. Get up and talk to them, right now!"

Willie crawled out of bed to take the call, and I marveled at how he instantly became sober. "Thank you, Sir," he said to the policeman on the phone. "I shall take care of the situation first thing in the morning. There's not much I can do at this hour, but thanks for informing me." He went back to bed and drifted off to sleep. This puzzled me. He seemed so unconcerned.

Later that morning he explained, "Your niece was driving the car (*without a license*) and was blinded by the lights of the oncoming traffic. She was afraid she would drive into the cars, so she turned the wheel sharply to the right and landed in a ditch full of water. We managed to climb out through the windows and proceeded to walk home, soaking wet. We stopped at a nearby farmhouse to ask for assistance and the owner could see we were a messy looking pair and came out with a shot gun . . . so we quickly moved on. A truck driver passing by, saw us walking the dark lonesome highway, and recognizing me, offered us a ride home. Don't worry, Jessie," he said, "I'll take care of everything. The car is wet but it will dry out. I have a tow truck ordered to do the job."

Too many times Willie drove home so drunk he couldn't get out of the car. He'd park on the street in front of our house and lean on the horn until Billy or Sandy and I would rush out and practically carry him in. It was embarrassing as all the neighbors could see and hear what was going on. He found no shame in his behavior. I wished, and often prayed that he would be arrested for drunken driving and spend a night in jail. That may have helped, but it never happened.

Parking on the street was not permitted between the hours of 2:00 a.m. and 4:00 a.m. for street cleaning, both winter and summer. Willie was too drunk to put the car in the garage and decided to take his chances. During the night, a young neighbor boy came home a little plastered and plowed into the back end of our Cadillac. The street was poorly lit and the car was black, so it was difficult for a bleary-eyed drunk to spot. The boy was scared and went home to tell his father that he drove into Mr. Masterson's car. The father came over and woke us up to ask us not to call the police, as the kid was drunk. He promised to pay the damages. Willie said, "Okay, no problem." However, the next-door neighbor heard the crash and saw the boy leave the scene of the accident, and reported it.

The next day the police were at our door. Willie said, "Oh, my wife was driving the car and she left it on the street. I was going to call you this morning and tell you all about it." I don't know all the details of the conversation Willie had with the Police, but they obviously didn't believe him. Several days later, I was called into police headquarters to give my side of the story. I was frantic, but Willie was shouting over my tears and told me to get down there and answer the questions, and he told me exactly what to say, and what not to say. I was so frightened, I was trembling. Daddy David's, "always tell the truth," came pounding through my mind, but my beloved husband was at the podium and he was preaching the sermon. I thought I had no choice but to obey.

I dressed carefully in my favorite navy-blue two-piece suit. I wore a white blouse, white shoes, and white costume jewelry. Chantilly perfume was the final touch before I drove to the police station, where I was seated before two officers, who cross-questioned me. I carefully fulfilled my obligation to cover Willie's lies.

The officers interrogated me back and forth, sometimes firing questions so fast I was getting confused. Willie told me this may happen, and I followed his advice to go silent and wait a few seconds before giving a reply, then ask politely if they would please repeat the question. They knew I had been prompted and felt sorry for me, and let me go after an hour of brutal cross questioning. I drove home totally shaken and cried for hours. When I finally ran dry of bitter tears, I faced reality and Willie, head on.

"I will never lie for you again Willie Masterson. Never! Don't even test the waters. It won't happen. I don't care what it will cost you, even if it costs you your life. I will never lie for you again, and that's a promise." I think he believed me, as I never had to face this kind of situation again.

***

Willie started telling lies. Maybe he was always telling lies and I just started catching on a little late. I don't know what load of turnips he thought I arrived on in this world, but some of his lies were so transparent, it was pathetic. Like telling me he would be home late tonight because he had to unload the Lady Leeside. That gave me the night off, so the kids and the dog and I decided to visit my mother, who lived on the other side of the river. As we were going over the Redwood Bridge, I saw the Lady Leeside traveling north, and it should have been sitting at dockside to the south, as per Willie's story. The next morning, I asked Willie when he got the boat off to head up North. "Oh, that was after midnight," he said. We both went uncomfortably silent. Once again, I didn't confront him, and let him get away with telling lies. This wasn't helping Willie. I was providing him with the freedom to continue hurting me and the family, but I didn't realize it.

There were several times when Willie arrived home by taxi or a friend – not sure which, and had no idea where his car was. The next day I would transport him around town to his local haunts, searching for his vehicle. There were times the location we found the car in was upsetting to me. The message was coming through loud and clear. I had to get out of this mess, but the escape route was not an easy one. I had two beautiful children to feed, clothe, educate, and provide a home for. I had limited skills, and no experience in the working world.

I had to fix that first. I registered for a correspondence course that took me two years to complete. Now I had my grade 12, but no experience and no references.

No one wanted to hire me. After hundreds of rejections, I finally got hired by a collection agency on straight commission. Willie left our house at 6:00 a.m. every morning and didn't arrive home again till late evening, so I was free to work without him knowing. I hired my two children to do essential chores, and they were delighted with the extra money I gave them. However, I wasn't making any. I was too soft. I worked every day, five days a week for three weeks, paying out good money for gas and collecting not a cent. Still, I wouldn't give up. I was determined to get 'experience.' It was the only way I could get out of this troublesome marriage.

The boss called me to his office. He had a stern look on his face. I think he wanted to fire me on the spot, but didn't have the heart to do that, to such a dedicated worker. He was holding a paper in his hand, and staring at it. Finally, he said, "You haven't been making any money Jessie, so I thought I'd give you a real opportunity. This fellow has owed me $3,000.00 for over three years, and refuses to pay. If you can collect this one, I'll pay you twenty percent commission."

Wow! That would be a month's wages, all in one crack. I was excited, and determined! I took the overdue statement and went home to dream of my success.

I was on the road bright and early next morning. I located the address where I was to make my collection, and with high expectations and determination, I entered the building. Lights were on but no sound was coming from any of the rooms. I walked quietly by each doorway and peered in to see if any living person was around. I checked several doors, then came to the last one, where I found more than I expected. The man in question was holding a young girl's legs up around his waist and kissing her passionately, while pulling her panties down and rubbing her bare buttocks. I was more than surprised. I was shocked! I yelled a healthy, loud, "Oh!" The man dropped the girl and she ran screaming down the hallway, yanking up her britches as she ran toward the bathroom, and closed the door.

"What the hell do you want?" the red faced individual asked.

"Just $3,000.00, and I'll be on my way," I said calmly, but firmly.

With shaking hands, he sat down at his desk and wrote the check out for me. I was now a successful bill collector. My boss couldn't believe my good fortune, and complimented me. "Congratulations, Jessie! How did you do it?"

I calmly replied, "You just have to be in the right place, at the right time."

***

It was early November and winter had already settled in. Willie was sent out to a wilderness camp in Northern Manitoba to run an ice fishing operation. They were carrying a plane load of fish and heading back to Winnipeg when they entered a cloud of ice crystals. The pilot looked out the window and realized his wing was just about touching the ice below, so he flipped the plane, and when he turned, the wing hit the ice and broke the tip off, and it hit the side of the cockpit. He flipped the plane back the other way, and broke the other wing off. The plane dropped down on the frozen lake, and broke the tail off. When the plane stopped moving, it didn't flip upside down or everyone would have been killed. Out of the five passengers only one man had a nose bleed.

As the plane was settling down on the ice, the wall of ice crystals cleared for a few minutes, just long enough for Willie to get his bearings. He spotted the Hydro line going across from the main shore to Hogan's Isle and this gave him direction, so he told his men to start walking right away as the weather was going to close in, and it was getting dark. Willie and two other men made the seventeen-mile hike into town, but two men couldn't make it. Willie sent a bombardier back to pick them up, along with the fish and whatever was salvageable. The plane was a total write-off.

Willie had nightmares for days after this accident and proceeded to drink the memories away. My heart softened, as I realized the dangers he faced, time and time again. Was it any wonder Willie drank? When confronted with the question of why he continued to work in these conditions, he always answered, "Someday the family business will be mine. I am working for my future."

***

Willie was a handsome young man who had lots of money to flash around, and drove a new expensive car every year. The female population had the hots for him and were eager to let me know it. They even had the nerve to phone me at home and say, "I'm in love with your husband, and I don't care if you know it or not. Why don't you just get lost? He doesn't love you anymore. He loves me and I love him."

The first phone call I received was devastating, but after receiving a few more like this, I simply said, "I'll take your number and when he decides which one of you ladies he wants to keep, I'll give you a call. I have five on the list so far." They'd hang up, perhaps to think about the competition they faced.

I didn't mention this to Willie. I guess I loved him because I suffered jealousy pains when the female world around him flirted and fell all over him. I hated him for how he reacted to them, lapping up their fondling and attention. I hated how he drank, yet I feared losing him, so I allowed him to use me as the proverbial doormat that alcoholics love to wipe their feet on. I didn't realize that I was allowing Willie to drink and ruin his life and mine.

***

Willie was out of town again, so I called a girlfriend and we decided to meet for dinner and a movie. Storm warnings on the radio were quite clear, but they weren't meant for me. I still planned to go to the movie with Judy. When we came out of the four-hour movie, the streets were blocked and traffic was at a stand-still. Buss's weren't operating. Taxi cabs were few and far between, and mostly occupied. We finally hailed one cab, who took Judy home, in the opposite direction from where I lived, and then headed for my address. Weather got worse by the minute. The only way the taxi could travel was to follow a snowplow that happened to be clearing the main street, going toward my home. We got within two long blocks of my destination and the snowplow turned east, but I needed to go west. The taxi driver called it quits. I had to walk the rest of the way. The snow was wet and deep. I was wearing short snow boots and nylon stockings and had to trudge through snow up to my knees. I soon became exhausted and lay down on the snowbank to rest. When I caught my breath, I decided the best way would be to crawl or roll over the top of the snow. I took turns rolling and crawling over the snow-covered sidewalk, all the way to my house. It took a long time, but I persisted and when I got there I found the snow had drifted up on the doorstep and I couldn't open the door. All I had were my hands to clear the snow away. It was a good thing it was warm out and I was young and strong, and had the will to see my kids again. That drove me to superpower and I got inside, exhausted, and thankful to be alive. The baby sitter lived next door and she managed to make it home safely.

***

Summer fishing season was over and Willie and one of his employees cleaned up things at the camp and headed for home in a whitefish boat. His freighter, Lady Leeside, had left ahead of him. The camp was now closed for the season.

Willie was resting uneasy and didn't know why. He decided to check his cargo to see if all was going well. He was shocked to see the gas drums he was transporting were on fire and ready to explode. He had to act quickly. He cut the ropes to the lifeboat, and he and his co-worker jumped aboard. They barely escaped when the boat blew up. Gas was burning on the water all around them. The lifeboat took on water when it was dumped overboard, and all they could find to bail the water out, was their rubber boots. The heat from the flaming waters that surrounded them, singed their hair, eyebrows, and eyelashes, but they were safe as they slowly drifted away from the terrifying inferno. They sadly watched the flames die a watery death as their only means of transportation vanished. The badly burned fishing boat sunk to it's watery grave at the bottom of Lake Winnipeg.

The captain of Lady Leeside saw the red reflection in the midnight sky and knew instinctively that Willie was in trouble. He turned the freighter around and went back to search and rescue the two men.

When Willie got home, he called his father. William Masterson only had one thing to say, "What the hell are you doing home." He was more concerned about the loss of the fishing boat than the ordeal his son had been through. It was only three drinking days before his father sent him out north again to another remote fishing station.

***

Back at home our heating bill was off the wall, so we had the insulation inspected. We found the house was made of scrap lumber, mostly rotten, and next to no insulation at all. The inside walls were plastered, and the exterior was stuccoed to cover up their shoddy work. We made the decision to put the house up for sale. The day after we moved out, the liquid air plant, located directly behind us, blew up and knocked all the plaster off the house, both inside and out.

We purchased a new home in the district of Westwood. It was close to several schools, but there wasn't a church nearby. There was a portable across the street from our home and someone decided to use it for a Sunday school. I sent the kids, but my son wasn't interested and opted for hockey or baseball. Sandy went faithfully until one day the teacher asked her to read from the bible. She had a reading disability that had not been detected at the time, and she stumbled over the difficult words. The teacher made a rude remark about how badly she read and Sandy was totally embarrassed. She broke down crying and threw the bible at the teacher and came home sobbing her heart out. I thought about the situation for a few minutes, then told Sandy it was wrong to throw the bible, but the teacher was wrong also in what she did. I told her she didn't have to go back there again, but we would attend a different church every Sunday until she found the one she liked. Each Saturday night we checked the newspaper for an interesting church to visit the next day. It became a real fun exercise.

One warm Sunday morning in Spring, we walked up to a big, beautiful, old stone church. Huge fluffy snowflakes were floating gently through the air as the church bells played a familiar hymn. It was beautiful beyond a doubt. It touched our hearts. That day, Sandy settled on Westminster United Church as her church, and we attended faithfully. Many years later she was married there.

Sandy wanted me to give her a driving lesson, so after church I took her to a quiet farm area where there was little or no traffic. I was teaching her to drive forward and backward at a good speed, just like I had been taught. It rained overnight and the road was greasy and she slid into the soft shoulder. She attempted to pull it back on the road, but it slid further into soft, greasy Manitoba gumbo. The back wheel sunk completely down to the rim. It was impossible to drive it out. We needed help. It was a lonely farm road with only one house in sight. In my Sunday best clothes, and high heeled shoes, I cut across the field, climbed over the fence, and headed toward the farmhouse to seek help. I was almost there when I spied a goat charging at full speed in my direction. I didn't know I could run that fast . . . till then. I made it to the farmhouse a millisecond before the goat. I was all puffed out and terrified, so I didn't take time to knock. I barged through the door of the farmhouse, into a very large kitchen. It had a huge homemade table in the middle of the floor and several farmhands were seated around it, having lunch. Not one person raised their head to acknowledge that I had burst into their dining area. Finally, with a huffing and a puffing I said, "The goat out there was chasing me and that's why I didn't take the time to knock on your door."

"Ya!" they chorused.

"I'm sorry but my car is stuck in the mud on the road out front, and I wondered if you could possibly pull me out."

"Ya!" That's all one fellow said, and kept on eating.

"So, you will come and help us?" I stammered. There was no answer and everyone kept on eating. I stood dumbfounded for another silent moment or two, then said, "Do you have a tractor?"

The man who seemed to be the boss, said, "Ya."

"I'll pay you for your trouble. I really need your help," I added in a pleading voice.

No one answered.

Thinking I was wasting my time, I thanked them and apologized for troubling them, and left. I looked around to see where the angry goat was, and felt relieved that it was nowhere to be seen. I started back across the field, worried and bewildered. I didn't know what to do. We were miles from the main street. Suddenly, out of nowhere, came a huge turkey, just a running and a flapping his wings. He wasn't happy to see me. Once again, I was doing a marathon. I practically flew across the field and over the fence with the turkey at my heels. As I landed on the other side of the fence, my shoe stuck in the soft earth, but I kept rolling forward. With one shoe on and one shoe off I backtracked to find my lost footwear. Now my shoeless foot was covered in muck, as well as my coat. I didn't have much choice, I put my muddy shoe on and continued the walk to the car. I got back safely, but winded, and told Sandy the bad news. "I don't think they are going to help us. We'll have to wait for some traffic to come this way and that could be a long time, or one of us must walk back to the main highway and locate a phone. First, I must rest a bit. After my encounter with those unfriendly farm creatures, I'm shaking and exhausted."

My heart was pounding. I was concerned. I didn't want to leave Sandy in the car by herself and I didn't want her to walk the lonely road alone either. I was deep in worrisome thought when suddenly I heard a tractor coming around the back of the farmhouse. I breathed a sigh of relief! Help was coming after all.

Two men came, hooked up the car, pulled it out and left without saying a word or even looking our way.

It was a relief to be back on the road again. Today's driving lesson was canceled.

***

Willie was advised by his father that he was to fly to his next appointment, 550 miles north of Winnipeg, to manage another fish Camp. He was told he would find excellent living quarters, and everything he needed was already there. In the meantime, the pilot was told by Mr. Masterson to unload Willie and his helper, plus grocery supplies, on a rock nearby and not to let the men see the cabin, because they wouldn't stay.

Willie and Stanley, his helper, walked as per directions, carrying meager supplies to their winter lodging. It was a small log shack, and you could put your hand between the logs. This was a camp they were to live in all winter, in -50-degree weather. It had mud floors and one wooden bunk bed in the middle of the room . . . with no mattresses. They took some fishnets and threw them across the bunks and made mattresses out of them. There was a tin heater in one corner and an old wood burning stove in the opposite corner . . . that was it.

The men took one look at the establishment, then gazed up at the sky to watch the company plane gradually disappear.

Willie and Stanley got busy and gathered moss from the bush and chinked in between the logs, covering it with snow, then watered it down to ice it in.

They were promised to be back home by Christmas, but when December twenty-one rolled around they knew they had been forgotten, so they decided to strike out on their own. Enough was enough! The next morning, they got up to put their boots on, and found they were frozen to the floor. They managed to get them loose, and started their forty-five-mile walk to Oak Leaf Lake, hoping to catch the mail bombardier going into Walterton town, but they just missed it and it was the last one before Christmas. They hired a man to take them to meet the Churchill train, but found it wasn't coming through for two days. Willie and Stanley hit the beer parlor and got pickled. They eventually caught the train and arrived in Winnipeg the morning of December the twenty-fourth. Willie was ordered out of town on Boxing Day, December twenty-six, but he refused to go unless they were supplied with a bombardier and lumber to make a floor in their living quarters and lining for the walls. A bombardier was sent out, but it needed new rubber tracks. The parts were flown in and Willie and his partner installed them. They had never done this sort of thing before, but they tackled it and got it done.

They had two carloads of fish to transport before the season was over, then stop to square up with the Hudson Bay manager before heading to Hudson House. They burned a wheel bearing and had to cut one of the wheels off. They threw it inside and ran on three wheels, all the way to Hudson House. They had to wait five days for the airplane to come to take them home. They remained drunk the whole time. When the plane arrived, the pilot said, "I have orders to keep you here and put you to work." Willie and Stanley refused to work, and got on the plane and wouldn't leave. They were finally taken back to Winnipeg.

Willie told his father he was not going back there again. Mr. Masterson was not happy about his son's decision and promptly left his cozy warm office, drove to his beautiful home in an upscale neighborhood, in his top of the line Cadillac, and mentally tried to solve his problem with several glasses of rye whiskey and water, which he shared with his wife. Willie's parents were unknowingly paving a visible platform for alcoholic problems to take root.

**

Willie said, "Jessie, I want you to dress in your finest, as I'm taking you and the whole family out to dine in the most expensive restaurant in town. Important dignitaries will be attending and Dad and I want to impress them. They have loads of money," he explained with a great deal of excitement, "and we want their business."

Twenty-six well-dressed family members and executive type people were seated in one of Winnipeg's high-class restaurants. Candles flickered along the snow-white linen table cloths, as the guests viewed the interesting menu. Willie ordered drinks for everyone. This would surely impress the best of the best. He ordered a rye and water for me, knowing I wouldn't drink it, but it looked good. After he finished his drink he switched our glasses. He was drinking two to one around the table. Orders were placed for our meals, and that took a little time to prepare, so drinks were ordered once again.

Willie was starting to slur, but had no trouble directing his lips to the glass he was holding. Other people were taking their time but Willie was downing the drinks like there was no tomorrow. The waitress could see Willie was becoming disorderly and ignored his several calls for refills. The next time she passed his way he ran his hand up her leg and called her 'Sweetheart.' That did it! She called management, and Willie was asked to leave. His twenty-five guests followed. Everyone but me, found it hilarious to be kicked out of this upscale restaurant.

"Don't worry folks," Willie said cheerfully, "the day is not lost. We shall gather at the Red River race track. We can have a fine meal there and have a bit of fun as well, betting on the horses."

This was another new adventure for me. I'd never been to a race track. I was told to pick a horse and go to the wicket and pay two dollars. I could handle that. I looked the pamphlets over and saw a horse running called Blunderbust, with odds 38 to 1. With my warped way of thinking, I thought 38 to 1 sounded like a sure bet. I purchased my ticket.

Mrs. Masterson asked, "What horse did you bet on, Deary?" and when I told her she said, "Now that was foolish! You just threw your hardworking husband's money away. That horse will never come in. It's called a long shot." She strutted off to join more intelligent racing fans. I was totally embarrassed!

The horses came out of the gate. Blunderbust looked like he was running the race alone as he was half a track ahead of the other horses. The crowd was roaring. There was hysteria in the air. My mother-in-law came running back and threw her arms around me. "Your horse is winning! Your horse is winning! I can't believe this. You will win a lot of money!"

Blunderbust was coming around the corner at home stretch and was running so fast he couldn't make the corner. He slipped and fell, breaking his leg. He was taken away in an ambulance. I felt sorry for the poor horse, but understood that I had a lot to learn about horse races and life in general.

We started for home and because Willie had consumed far too much liquid refreshment, he decided to take the perimeter around the city, for our homeward journey. It was dark and lonely with very little traffic. About the loneliest spot along the route, Willie pulled to the side of the road and tried to rape me. That didn't go over well with me. I fought him like a tiger and would have happily walked home if I could get out of the car. He ripped my beautiful dress down the front and was acting like a grizzly bear in heat. I couldn't believe what was happening. I got in several good punches and kicks and was twisting his ears into oblique configurations when the lights of a car caressed the windshield. Willie straightened up.

The car stopped beside us. It was the police. "Are you having trouble?" they asked.

Willie answered in an amazingly sober voice, "All is well officer. Just necking with my wife."

They smiled and drove off, so did we, and not one word was spoken for the remainder of the trip home. I silently sobbed as we traveled homeward. I couldn't believe my husband would act like this. He became a person I didn't know, but I realized liquor was dictating his violent and disgusting behavior.

***

Willie arrived home from work one day, happily drunk and announced he bought lake front property, 120 miles north of Winnipeg. He bought it sight unseen, over a few glasses of rye whiskey and water. With much excitement, we traveled out to see this wonderful purchase.

A business associate purchased the lot for us, and was there to point out where our surveyor posts were located. We fought our way through the tangle of brush and fallen trees. There were many beautiful white birch and mountain ash trees on the lot. These would be saved when we cleared the land.

The following week, Willie brought out a small gang of men to clear an area for the cottage, and a small spot farther back in the bush where the outhouse would be built. The underbrush was taken to the sandy beach to be burned. Once the lot was ninety percent cleared we could see the outhouse was smack in the middle of the yard. That was promptly moved to a more discrete location.

We worked diligently during the day and drove 40 miles west to Willie's cousin's home for the evening. This worked well for us, as we had the use of their shower and comfortable sleeping quarters and could return to our beach front property the next day, refreshed and ready for another hard day's work.

A huge cottage, our neighbors referred to as 'The Hotel,' finally emerged. It had four bedrooms, a large living room, spacious kitchen and a small dressing room, or nighttime relief area. The building had a forty-eight-foot veranda facing the lake, which would eventually accommodate another four beds. Before it was completed or even livable, Willie was busy inviting guests to come out for a weekend.

This cottage project was a blessing for the kids and the dog, as it got them out of the city where problems lurk to entice active little minds, but it was an extra workload for me. It was like keeping two houses and yards in shape, but I didn't complain. I enjoyed the construction stages of the cottage. There was the working togetherness, the anticipation of the future, along with fresh air, peace and quiet, and drinking was done only after the working day was over.

The most noise to be heard in this location was from the odd car rumbling past on the gravel road or the screeching of a large gray owl perched on top of a birch tree. He didn't seem to appreciate us invading his territory, and I think he was warning us of a troubling future. He gave us constant warnings with his hooting, and swooping dangerously over us. This scared the children out of their wits. I wasn't comfortable with the bird attacking us either.

Our son Billy made a beautiful sign in woodcraft at school. It was a pair of owls and three baby owls with one baby hanging upside down. We attached this to a large driftwood log and placed it at the entrance of our lot, which we now called 'Hooterville'.

There wasn't much traffic on the road that passed our cottage, but any car that did come by, usually stopped. It seemed Willie knew every truck driver in the area. The truckers knew the stop was good for a drink or two on good old Willie.

It was the fifth week of ownership and we headed out to our campsite as usual. We were loaded with essentials, such as pots of chili and stew to feed the workers, bread, butter, beans, toilet paper, pop, and mosquito repellent etc. It was a cold miserable weekend and we worked with our winter jackets on. Mosquitoes were out in full force, causing a great deal of discomfort. Clearing the underbrush was hard work and the physical labor kept us warm. A bonfire on the sandy beach was handy if we required more heat or comfort.

A make-shift table was constructed from planks and trusses, and a Coleman stove was set up to make hot coffee and warm the stew. Paper plates made clean up easy. We simply chucked the used plates on the bonfire.

I was busy preparing the midday meal at one end of the plank table when I heard a strange noise. There, on the other end of the plank was a busy little squirrel opening a loaf of our bread. He cleverly pulled the paper open at the seam and took a slice and scampered off before I realized what was happening. Our dog Nicki took after the squirrel but he was no match for its agility.

The following week we were struggling with fiberglass insulation, placing it between the joists in the cottage. It was a dirty job and made our skin itch. I was anticipating a nice hot bath come evening, when I noticed a car pull up in our driveway. It was our neighbors from across the back lane in Winnipeg. Willie invited them to visit and they took him up on it. They were here for the weekend and we had no place to house them. The cottage had no windows or doors. I'll just have to tell them we can't accommodate them, I decided. They will simply have to return home and come to visit us when the cabin is finished.

When I explained the predicament to our neighbors, they said, "Gee, we like roughing it! We don't mind. We have sleeping bags, and you have a roof to keep the rain off. That's all we need."

The menfolk got busy and covered the walls and windows with plastic sheeting. Mosquitoes were swarming around in thick black clouds, so they covered the rafters and doors as well. A loose plastic sheet was draped over the main door and a heavy sleeping bag was nailed over the plastic. This kept the heat in and the mosquitoes out. The room was a complete vacuum, but it was cold, so they brought our big barbecue inside and built a coal fire in it. They topped the fire with green grass to create smoke to drive the mosquitoes out. After the mosquitoes were gone, they stoked up the coals to provide some heat. We were concerned about keeping the children warm, but we really didn't have to worry about that, they were busy running and chasing one another in fun and games.

I brought the Coleman inside to cook a meal for my family and our visitors. They weren't fancy folk and were content with pork and beans, bread, and butter, and lots of cake and cookies.

Everyone was fed and Katelyn and I were cleaning up and putting things away. We put all the kids to bed in the back bedroom with their sleeping bags on the floor and they thought it was great fun. There were a pair of three-year-old twins, plus five other children, including my own. They tossed around for a short time but soon fell fast asleep.

Suddenly, I was having a difficult time focusing or functioning. I had to give in. A terrible feeling came over me. I struggled with my feelings but simply couldn't stand it any longer. "I'm sorry folks, I'm not feeling well. My head is aching and I feel sick to my stomach. I have to go to bed." I apologized and headed off to my room and flopped across our make-shift bed. I passed out!

Our visitors, Geoffrey and Katelyn stayed up and visited with Willie, sitting around the bar-B-Que smoking, and drinking for about an hour. Then Katelyn said, "I have a headache too. Does Jessie have any aspirins?"

"Sure," Willie replied," There's some in her purse over there," and he pointed to the far wall where my purse was hanging from a nail.

Katelyn proceeded to cross the room and fell flat on her face. She passed out! Immediately Geoffrey and Willie knew what was wrong. "It's carbon monoxide poisoning! They need air! "Open the windows, quick!" Willie shouted.

They immediately removed the coal burning bar-B-Que and opened windows and doors to let fresh air in. All the oxygen had been driven out by the smoke, and the coal gas took over.

Geoffrey and Willie took turns waking the children. It wasn't easy. When they got a small response they went to the next victim. Then they came to me. I was in a different universe. I was floating. I didn't have a care in the world. I could hear them call my name and it annoyed me. Why didn't they leave me alone? All I wanted to do was sleep. Oh, peaceful sleep. Go away! Go away! Go away, was all I could think of, as I floated around in a state of unconsciousness. Leave me alone! Don't bother me! Can't you see how tired I am? I'm comfortable here. Don't you understand?" Finally, I gave a grunt and they left me for a while and went back to rousing the children, one by one. Each time they came back to me it was another difficult time to get me to respond, but they didn't give up. I don't know who kept working on me, but someone did . . . probably Geoffrey. I finally came to, as fresh air flooded the room, but I had no strength to get up or move my body.

All three adults and seven children came out of this ordeal just fine, but I couldn't stand on my feet for over a week. Willie had to carry me out to the car and prop me up on pillows on the back seat for the drive home. No one realized how close to death I was. No one thought of getting medical attention for me. It was a near fatal accident that could have wiped out two families. If Katelyn hadn't fallen on the floor, no one would have realized the seriousness of the situation. They would have all gone to bed, never to wake up again.

As we drove away from the cottage that day, the wise old owl hooted at us from his vantage point at the top of the tall silver birch tree. He seemed to be saying, "This is a lesson city folk better remember."

***

The cottage was finally completed that summer, and we were inundated with visitors every weekend, thanks to Willie's constant invitations.

Geoffrey and Katelyn thought the area was ideal for their family and purchased the lot next to ours. The near tragic weekend they spent with us didn't hinder their enthusiasm for outdoor activities and roughing it.

Visitors came in droves and the parties roared on. All I did was clean, cook, mix drinks and empty dirty ash trays. Card games often went on all night and I was summoned to cook breakfast for all.

As soon as the children were home from school, we left for the cottage. As we traveled along the lonely dusty gravel road we noticed a group of tiny baby pheasants. I stopped the car to have a closer look. They were so beautiful! Billy ran to pick one up and out of the bushes came the protective mother. She charged at each of us in turn, making us flee for cover. I couldn't blame her for that.

Farther along I spied wild raspberries shining brightly in the sunlight. We stopped and ate to our enjoyment. Oh, how delicious they were! We probably would have picked more berries but I didn't have anything to put them in, besides our tummies. After we had our fill we went back to the car. When I started the engine, the roar of the motor broke the silence of the wilderness and out popped a huge black bear from behind the bushes we had been stripping. He must have thought we were an interesting little group and simply watched us as we devoured his evening meal. Judging from his size, I would estimate the beast to be about 400 pounds. I drove away quickly and never again considered stopping along that lonely highway. I just thank God there were lots of berries that summer and the bear wasn't hungry.

***

My eighty-three-year-old mother was anxious to see our cottage, so plans were made to take her, my sister-in-law and a couple of nieces out for a few days. Mother was delighted with everything, especially the wild flowers and proceeded to dig some up to take back to her home. I noticed her with a spade in hand, traveling down the road and curiosity urged me to follow her. She was about to dig up a neighbor's flower bed. Granted, it did look like they were growing wild because of the massive growth of weeds and grass surrounding them. Gently I hustled her back to the safety of our yard.

A neighbor who lived farther up this lonesome highway invited us to come to visit. Her cottage was on the west side of the lake, about sixty winding, dusty miles from our cottage and very close to 'the end of the earth.' It was July 1968 and my thirteen-year-old daughter and her two teenage cousins were bored to tears, and the adults were too polite to admit they felt the same. A suggestion to go to a new and different place added a touch of excitement to an otherwise humdrum day. I packed the three teenagers in the back seat, and my mother and sister-in-law squashed themselves in beside me in the front seat of my 1966 Pontiac Stata Chief, that I affectionately called 'Old Betsy', and we headed down the dusty road.

There was nothing but straggly stunted pine trees and swamp willows to view along the never-ending miles of wilderness that city folk would probably enjoy. If we were lucky, mother nature would provide us with a view of a magnificent creature, such as a black bear, or a deer, a hawk or owl, but this day was too hot even for wild life to make an appearance. We traveled slowly along the narrow gravel road, admiring the beauty of the cloudless sky and the nearness of God, when suddenly an old car came roaring up from behind, passing us in a hurricane cloud of dust. Three bare chested men were hanging out of the windows from the waist up, flailing their arms in the wind and shouting obscenities as they passed. When it registered on his brain that our car was full of women traveling this highway to nowhere, the driver slammed on the brakes. Both cars burned rubber and skidded to an abrupt stop. The inebriated men jumped out of their vehicle and their swaying bodies, distorted faces, and frothing mouths, came rushing toward us.

"Lock the doors and hold on to your hats!" I shouted to my panic-stricken passengers, as I shifted 'Old Betsy' into reverse and took off in a bit of a tail spin. The car swerved and raised a thick cloud of gritty air, as I skilfully moved my trusty vehicle away from the assailants. With a steady hand on the wheel, I kept the car in the middle of the road, spewing a fan of gravel left and right. Old Betsy was built like a tanker and hugged the road well. I was thankful for that, as I pressured the car to make some distance between us and the enemy. My passengers were either frozen in fear or duly respectful of the driving talent of the 'back up artist'. There wasn't a sound from anyone, but I could hear my breathing pacing itself and my heart thudding within my breast.

I was good at driving in reverse, thanks to my brother Ray. He made me drive backward and forward at the same speed over and over and over when I was learning to drive. He said, "If my sister is going to drive, she is going to be a good driver." Even though I paid for professional lessons, that extra training was certainly valuable, and I was now putting it to good use.

The smell of swampy pine mixed with stagnant ditch water, burned my nostrils. I could only see as far as the next bend in the road, but my mind zeroed in to total concentration. It was fight or flight, driving in reverse. The welfare of all of us was at stake! My only ammunition was a clear mind and gut instinct.

The men stopped running and staggered back to their car. They drove off and disappeared.

"They could be waiting around the next bend in the road," I said to my frightened family. "I don't trust them. We'll wait here for a while and give them time to depart, since there is no place to turn around." Old Betsy wasn't easy to navigate. It had manual transmission (Armstrong steering) and needed a strong arm to maneuver it. The road was narrow and ditches were deep on both sides and full of dirty water, mosquitoes, and frogs. I knew it would take several attempts to slowly turn this big car around in the middle of the road and the attackers could be upon us before I could get moving in the direction I wanted to go. It was best to continue our journey and hopefully find a turnaround point. Periodically there were logging trails leading off the main road, but they were few and far between. I could turn around on one of them, but the assailants could also be hiding there, ready and waiting for us. It was a dilemma.

We stopped for ten minutes before continuing. I drove slowly and cautiously with my eyes peeled ahead for any danger signs. As we made our way around the next bend, I spied the car ahead of us. I stopped! I shifted into reverse and backed up a safe distance and waited once again. I hoped for another car to come along and I would follow it, but no such luck. After a thirty-minute wait, I decided to try again. Cautiously I drove around the bend in the road. This time the car was gone. We breathed a sigh of relief, yet I remained alert, watching for any sign of that carload of trouble. Everything was quiet, except for the sound of the tires on the dry gravel road. Conversations became light and happy again.

We passed a logging trail but there seemed to be no need to turn back now, so we continued. We traveled several miles when I noticed a car in the rear-view mirror, and my heart skipped a beat. A black car was coming at a tremendous speed. "That's them!" I cried. "They must have hidden on that logging trail we passed and are now approaching us from behind. Well, I have news for them! They aren't getting a chance to cut us off, or attack us. I won't let them pass! They won't even get close. They can eat my dust!"

When the car came close enough, I put my strategy in high gear. I swayed the car back and forth, from one side of the road to the other, back, and forth, back, and forth, in a rhythmical fashion. The car behind me blasted its horn but I paid no attention. I concentrated on the miles ahead. Sway, sway, sway, skid, slip, and sway! It was a hair-raising experience for all of us. I couldn't tell what the car behind was doing as the dust I was raising made a thick security blanket between us. All I knew was, the driver was trying to pass me and I wasn't about to let him. We traveled together swaying and swerving and raising hell with highway, tires, and nerves, for thirty miles. Finally, our destination came in view. The trailing car was still close behind. I wheeled into my friend's driveway at top speed. The black car followed.

"Look at that! They have the nerve to follow us into the yard!" I exclaimed.

I was shaking vigorously but was no longer frightened as I knew my friends would protect me, at gunpoint if necessary. I jumped out of the car to face them.

Someone jumped out of the black car too, and hollered at me.

"Where the Hell did you learn to drive, lady?"

My mouth fell open in disbelief! I was speechless! It was the friend we were planning to visit.

***

A warm summer wind whipped the waves into frothy whitecaps in front of our cottage. The clear blue sky over my head accented the distant gathering dark clouds, forecasting the possibility of a storm, but for now all was pleasantly peaceful. Willie was working in town and wouldn't be here till Friday night, so I had some time for me to relax and enjoy a peaceful moment. The neighbor's noisy children and my daughter Sandy went to the park, a mile south of our cottage, because they were bored. Other than swimming, there was little to do at the beach, so this was a change of scenery for them and a peaceful moment for me. Relaxing on the soft sandy beach was a rare moment in my life. I closed my eyes and soaked in the warm July sunshine, closing my mind to the world. Suddenly I heard a familiar voice urgently calling my name.

"Mrs. Masterson, Mrs. Masterson, come quickly! Sandy is hurt," she cried out. It was our neighbor's teenage daughter Allison, running toward me, shouting and out of breath.

I bolted upright! "What's the matter? What happened?" I asked with concern.

"Sandy was swinging really high on the swing and suddenly the chain broke and threw her to the ground. She can't get up and she is crying in pain. I think she broke her leg. You must come right away to help her."

I ran to the cottage, grabbed my purse and keys and Allison hopped in the car beside me. I was in a state of minor shock as I drove to the little park. I stopped the car abruptly and ran to Sandy's side. She was lying on the ground in excruciating pain and there was no possible way for me to help her. I was frantic. I momentarily panicked. The only help available was a little group of children ages five to fourteen. With no phone in the area, I had to find help another way. I told the kids to stay with Sandy and talk to her and try to comfort her while I stopped the first car that comes along.

Thankfully, it wasn't long before a van appeared. I stood in the middle of the road waving my arms frantically making it impossible to pass without running over me. They had to stop. A middle-aged couple occupied the van, and looked quite perplexed at my actions. I explained the urgency but they were unresponsive. I wasn't about to let them leave. I was crying and pleading for their help. Finally, they followed my directions and pulled into the park where my daughter lay in distress.

Sandy was an average sized girl for her age, about 5' 6" tall and certainly weighed over 100 pounds. Somehow, we had to lift her into the car and take her to the hospital at Battleship Bay, approximately 50 miles away. This task was seemingly impossible.

The gentleman from the van suggested, "we must find a board and lift her onto it. That way we can carry her to the van and slide the board in . . . but we had no board.

One of the little boys said he saw a board in the ditch over yonder, so we went to investigate. Sure enough, there was a half sheet of warped plywood in the dirty ditch water, about as filthy green as one could imagine, but it was just what we needed right now. We pulled the board out of the water, and with many helping hands we gathered grass and scrubbed the surface as clean as we could.

The next task was to lift Sandy onto the board.

There was no time for friendly innuendos, so we didn't even introduce ourselves. There were more pressing issues at hand, so I can't tell you who the kind people were who thankfully took charge. For now, I'll call them Mr. and Mrs. Helper.

Mr. Helper gave instructions. "Everyone must get involved. Each one must hold a part of the body, and we will all lift together. I will take the upper part which is heaviest. My wife and this girl's mother will hold the broken leg, and the older children will handle the good leg. When I say lift, we all lift together. I want this young fellow over here to push the board under as we lift her off the ground," he said as he pointed to fourteen-year-old Lenny.

"Everyone, get your hands in place and ready to do your part. This won't be easy on any of us, and certainly not on Sandy, so pay attention and give all the strength you've got. Are we ready? One, two, three, lift!"

Sandy screamed a mighty scream, but we managed to lift her onto the board . . . now to get her into the van.

Mr. Helper backed his vehicle up as close as possible to the makeshift stretcher and we lifted her into the van. Sandy was in terrible pain, but I assured her help was on its way. I locked my car and left it at the park to be picked up later. It was the least of my concerns.

Uninvited, I crawled into the back of the van with my daughter and held her hands, trying to console her and convince her that she would be looked after soon.

The gravel road did not lend to a smooth ride, and with each bump, Sandy screamed. Each scream cut through my heart like a butcher's knife. The road seemed endless, and I felt so helpless. Tears poured down my cheeks, soaking my blouse, but I wouldn't let go of her hands to wipe them away. I had nothing to offer my child to ease her pain and suffering, and that was devastating. The fifty miles to the hospital, felt like it was 2000 light years away.

Mr. and Mrs. Helper didn't utter a word, during the whole fifty miles. We finally reached the hospital and Sandy was taken in on our makeshift stretcher for examination. The medical staff on duty couldn't do much to help her as they had no x-ray equipment. She would have to go to Winnipeg. They gave her a shot of morphine for pain and put her back in the van.

Heartsick, we traveled on. We hadn't gone far when the dark clouds I spotted earlier in the day, came directly overhead. Sheets of rain poured from above, then hail the size of mothballs came thundering down. The windshield wipers couldn't handle the deluge, and Mr. Helper had no choice but to pull to the side of the road and wait for the storm to pass. Thankfully, the morphine eased Sandy's pain for the moment and she lay quiet on her filthy wooden bed.

Manitoba storms don't often last long and this one was no exception. It was over in ten to fifteen minutes, leaving the pavement wet with puddles on the sides. When Mr. Helper attempted to pull back onto the highway the vehicle felt strange. He stopped to check his tires. He had a flat and the spare was underneath Sandy. We had another hurdle to jump. She had to be lifted out of the van to retrieve the spare and other equipment that was needed to change the tire. We need help! We had no choice, we waved at cars to stop to help us. Dozens passed before one kind soul pulled over to assist. They willingly came forth and helped pull Sandy out on her smelly dirty board and placed her gently on the side of the road, then helped to change the tire and put her back in the van.

More no-name helpers, but they were a blessing, and certainly appreciated by all concerned.

We were traveling once more, this time toward Manitoba General Hospital, an additional 50 miles away. What a relief to finally pull into emergency. She was placed on a nice clean stretcher and wheeled into admitting. Mr. and Mrs. Helper were thanked and relieved of their duties and could continue to their residence to ponder what happened next to the girl they rescued.

Nothing ever happens fast when you're suffering, and pains were returning viciously to Sandy's leg. The morphine was wearing off. After a lengthy routine of questions and answers they determined that Sandy, being thirteen years old, did not belong in the general hospital. She had to be admitted in the children's hospital. Her stretcher was then wheeled underground for a lengthy ride to the proper location. It took forever to have her placed in a hospital bed, and when she was, her head reached the headboard and her feet touched the foot board. She barely fit in. Sandy was wheeled off to the x-ray department and the conclusion was her leg was broken in three places. They called it a green break, like the way a green tree would tear, all jagged. It was not a clean break. This made repairing more delicate.

I knew an exceptionally good bone specialist who did the kind of work needed for my daughter's injury and I specifically asked if I could have this doctor do the job. I was assured I could. They couldn't operate immediately because of the morphine that the country hospital at Battleship Bay administered, to relieve her immediate pain. Sandy was scheduled for surgery the next morning. I stayed all night with my daughter and saw her off to the operating room early the next morning. I waited patiently for her to come back repaired and feeling better . . . that didn't happen. She was still suffering. They gave her pain killers and said it would just take time, that didn't happen either. She remained in painful distress all night. By morning, I was fit to be tied. I ordered the nurses to get the doctor back on the job. It wasn't long till they came to roll her back into surgery. They reset the leg again. Still she remained in excruciating pain. They filled her with pain killers that didn't work and scolded her for complaining. Another night was spent watching her suffer. Once again, I called for the doctor to come to her aid. Once again, she was taken to the operating room and the leg was re-set . . . still no improvement. This didn't add up in my estimation. Why was she going through this torture again and again? Then the thought came to me . . . I hadn't seen Dr. Whelply. I saw no sign of him. I wondered if he did the operation, or if an intern had done it, so I asked to talk to him personally.

The nurses came to prepare Sandy for yet another visit to the O.R. I wasn't about to let her go for another operation until I saw Dr. Whelply, and I told them so.

"You can't hold up the operating room," I was told.

"That's what you think!" I replied with determination. You just watch me! She's not going though that operating room door until I see the doctor I requested. So far, I haven't seen him, and I was told he was going to do the job." The nurses did an about turn and walked briskly away.

A few minutes later, two interns approached me. In their most dignified, professional voices, they said, looking over the top of their glasses, "We have run into a bit of difficulty with the setting of the breaks in your daughter's leg and we must take her into the operating room once again, I'm sorry."

"She's not going through those doors until I see my doctor," I told them firmly.

"You know, Mrs. Masterson, we are fully qualified doctors with many hours of practice to our credit, and there's no reason for you to be concerned. It will just take time for us to get your daughter comfortable, and on and on they went, explaining their qualifications and expertise.

I was not impressed.

"I really don't care who or what you interns are, you aren't touching my daughter again. No one is going to operate on her except Dr. Whelply, and that's final."

"But the operating room is scheduled for her right now. You can't hold up the operating room."

"Yes, I can, and I will! Don't you dare come near my daughter!"

They were insulted and walked away reluctantly.

I dashed to the nurse's station and went behind the desk to pick up the phone to call Willie.

The nurse said, "You can't come behind here, and you can't use that phone!"

"Really," I said, as I ignored her and phoned my husband. I told him to come to the hospital, right now! I hung up before he found an excuse to not come, and before the nurse could throw me out. Within ten minutes Willie was there. I could smell liquor on him but at least he was there to support me. I explained the situation to him, and we sat on either side of Sandy's bed and guarded her for over two hours.

Dr. Whelply finally arrived, out of breath, running into the room. "What's the matter Mrs. Masterson?"

"Nothing, Doctor. Everything is fine now that you are here."

Dr. Whelply wheeled Sandy into the O.R. and within forty-five minutes he rolled her out and she was without pain. She went home the next day, with a cast from the top of her leg to her toes. For nine long month's she struggled with the clumsy heavy cast and crutches, but she fully recovered. Walking flights of stairs at school and carrying books was a challenge, but her classmates were helpful most of the time.

Sandy had a lot of friends before her accident, but when she could no longer join in with their activities she was slowly cast aside, and became a lonely teenager. I heard of a cake decorating course being offered in the school across the street from our house and thought it might entertain her. I asked if she would like to go. She said "okay." I wanted to take the course and I knew Willie would not be pleased, but assisting Sandy became my passport to the course. Sandy found it a breeze and she outdid the instructor in many ways, in the first lesson. She certainly outdid me. The instructor said she was a natural. This was the beginning of a lifetime hobby for her. She made many prize-winning cakes and made a lot of friends and side money as well. She entered seven cakes in a competition and took six prizes. She is always in demand for her friendly advice and expertise. I doubt if the day will ever come that Sandy will give up expressing her artistic talent.

Sometimes we don't understand why things happen, but often they open doors to greater success. Because of the heavy cast on her leg, there were many activities Sandy was unable to take part in, but she found a hobby that filled her future with joy and personal satisfaction.

I guess her accident was a part of life's master plan.

***

To own a beautiful lake front cottage overlooking pristine waters is many a man's dream, and for our two children, Billy and Sandy, and Nicki our Samoyed dog, it was freedom to explore nature, spend hours in the water, and enjoy a safe, worry free life. It was a peaceful haven away from the drinking crowds, except on the weekends. There was such an abundance of nothing in this area that no one expected anything tragic to ever disrupt the tranquility.

Our family had a rigid routine. We arrived at the cottage Friday night, left for home Sunday evening before dark, carting all the dirty clothes, towels and bedding back for the weekly laundry. The cottage remained empty from Sunday night to Friday evening. The pattern was easy to follow for those with ill intent. But nothing ever happened here. Right!

Our son was sixteen years old, going on seventeen, and wished to have some grown up time at the cottage with his friend Norman. When he asked permission to spend Monday to Friday alone at the lake, my unequivocal reply was, "No way! That's no place to spend time alone at your age. There's no phone, no police protection, no emergency facilities of any kind . . . should you ever need it."

I guess all Mothers are worry warts by nature, and I was no exception. Chilling fear traveled like a lightning bolt through my veins, at the thought of my son and his friend spending time at our beach home alone. I noticed Norman was a small boy, about half the size of Billy, so he wouldn't be much of a defender, but that wasn't the biggest objection that came to mind. Fear targeted my personal world after hearing disturbing news on the radio. It felt too close to home for comfort.

"I don't like the idea of you boys being out there alone. It's not that I don't trust you, because I do. It's just a fear that something might go wrong. You might need help and there wouldn't be any. It's too isolated. Norman is welcome to come out any weekend he wishes."

Then Willie came on the scene. He said, "I think it's a good idea for the boys to go to the cottage alone. After all, they can legally drive a car, and not far from being of age to vote and do all sorts of adult things. You can't keep them tied down all their life," he said. "Of course, they can go. That's what the cottage is for."

I wasn't about to give up my worry platform. "I heard on the news this morning that two criminals escaped from Moody Mountain Penitentiary, and are considered dangerous. One is a convicted murderer. The other one was in for armed robbery. What if they show up at the cottage?" I strongly protested.

They laughed at my wild imagination, and I was out voted.

One escapee lived two cottages to the south of ours. I didn't like this boy, but he was a neighbor, so there wasn't much one could do about it. He had been at our cottage many times as he was close to my son's age, and he knew our pattern of living. He also knew we stored diesel fuel for our power plant, and handy tools and equipment in our shed. He witnessed us carrying in canned goods, liquor, and other supplies, so our place would be a prime place to target.

"Moody Mountain penitentiary is directly in line with our cottage, *(as the crow flies)* if you travel through swamp and bush all the way," I added in defense. "What if they should try that route and end up at our cottage, knowing they would have food and shelter at least for five days."

I was totally ignored and the boys made plans to go.

"When you get to the cottage, be sure to keep the doors locked," I instructed, to what I believed were deaf ears. "Don't carry all your money in your pocket or wallet. Keep a small amount so it looks legitimate but hide the balance of it. Also, hide your BB gun. It looks too much like the real thing, and hide the pellets too . . . just in case."

The boys laughed at my last-minute instructions and left for their five days of fun and freedom, but for some strange reason Billy heeded my advice. He hid his money and the pallets for his gun in the attic, which was accessed through the ceiling panel. Then they went about preparing their fishing gear for morning. It was still daylight, so they hadn't locked the cottage up yet.

Suddenly, two armed men burst through the door. One was carrying a homemade knife that was sharpened like a dagger, and the other had a gigantic crescent wrench. They were still wearing their prison clothes and looked mean. They threatened the boys with their weapons and proceeded to search their pockets for money and took what they had on them, plus the keys to our Billy's Austin Wolseley car. This was no social call.

They rummaged through the house for anything useful, and spotted the BB gun, which they took. They asked for more pellets but were told there were no more. They packed up all the food items they thought they could use, and a half bottle of whiskey, a few cans of beer, a supply of water and soft drinks.

They ordered the boys into the bedroom, ripped a flannelette sheet off the bed into strips, and tied them up. Their mouths were stuffed with parts of the flannelette sheet, so they couldn't talk or call for help. The boys wisely obeyed their every command.

Billy watched James Bond 007 Series a few nights before and one of the things they did when captured was to roll the tongue up so they couldn't push too much inside the mouth. They stiffened their bodies while being tied up, so after they relaxed there was a small amount of slack. They put this knowledge to good use. The flannelette sheets stretched a small amount, which was another added benefit. It wasn't much, but it was all they had to work with.

Norman was told to lie on the twin bed and Billy was tied to the lower part of the metal military bunk bed. They bound both boy's hands behind their backs and tied their ankles tightly together.

Nicki, our big friendly dog was with the boys, and he welcomed the criminals because he knew our neighbor's son. They patted the dog and played with him a short while, then locked him in the bedroom with the boys. They filled the dog's water dish, before leaving the boys to die. Without food or water for five days, it is unlikely the boys would have survived.

The captives remained tense, accepting their fate, and patiently waited. They didn't dare make a move until they knew the convicts were gone. They listened intently for the car engine to start and move on, which it eventually did, after they filled the car engine with diesel fuel from the shed, and after tearing out the back seat of the car and filling it with extra fuel, food, water and supplies they stole from the cabin.

At last the boys heard the sound they were patiently waiting for. The car took off, and the noise of the engine faded with distance. They waited about five minutes to be sure they were gone, then Billy started pushing against the wall to get his bed closer to Norman's bed, which was in the same room. Rolling back and forth, back, and forth, inching his way, he finally reached his friend. It took time, determination mixed with anger, and the desperate will to live, to finally reach his friend. They helped each other get untied and ran for help.

They ran with the dog to the nearest occupied cabin, which was approximately 1 1/2 miles west of our cottage. They frantically rapped on the door and asked for help. They told their story, but the people didn't know the boys, and didn't believe them.

"Get the hell off this property, right now, before I get my gun!" the angry male resident shouted! Devastated, but not defeated, the boys headed for town, which was a 40-mile walk, hoping perhaps a car might come down this seldom traveled highway and give them a ride to the police station.

The Goodall family had a cottage next door to ours, and they seldom spent a weekday at the lake, but something urged Geoffrey to drive out to his cottage that night. He recognized the boys walking on this lonely stretch of road and stopped. He had no reason to not believe every word they told him. He immediately transported them to the ranger's tower where they radioed the RCMP complete details of the incident, the license plate number, make and model of the car, plus the identity and description of the convicts. Road blocks were set up and the escapees were stopped before they got into Winnipeg proper. They were taken back into custody, but not before making a daring attempt to shoot the police with the BB gun.

The fugitives were originally from Moody Mountain Penitentiary, but after their capture they were taken to the high security prison in Kingston, Ontario to serve the balance of their terms.

Innocent victims seem to always pay a price, for they are left with scars in their memory chamber, forever. With the passage of time, details fade, but are never completely erased. This happened in 1968, but nightmares still emerge every now and then from the depths of the past, to remind us of the evils of the world that lurk around unexpected corners of everyday life. We should always count our blessings, but carry a big stick.

Thankfully our boys were safe at home again and life went back to normal . . . almost. Billy's car was impounded for two weeks. It was a minor inconvenience, but there was always Mom's car to borrow. I was happy that was all I had to forfeit.

"I believe divine intervention played a part in the rescue of my son and his friend. What happened was tragic but there are so many things that thankfully didn't happen, for nothing can replace the life of a child. Thank God, we still have Norman and my precious son.

That was enough for me. I was fed up with all the accidents, scary moments, endless work, the cooking, and cleaning and waiting on spongers, and the constant weekend drinking. I refused to go to the cottage anymore, so it was put up for sale. Without the cottage, there was no place to party, but alcoholics always manage to find a way.

***

We stayed around home a lot that summer and did some visiting with family and friends. We are both from large families so there was always somewhere to go and party, and drink.

Willie found another lake front property that was for sale, much closer to home. It was a former wheat field, so it had no trees on the property. That was no problem. We could plant our own trees and shrubs. It had a beautiful long sandy beach the length of the wheat field. On one end of the property there was an access road that led down to the Lake, and a small creek cut across a portion of the road. It was ideal for docking a boat. Willie and I looked it over and between us we decided to purchase the land and subdivide it into beach lots. It would be a terrific investment. We decided to build a cottage for ourselves on the corner lot, just off the access road. This was near a small town and not in wilderness like Hooterville was. We were excited about purchasing this property. I was especially thrilled to be included in the decision.

The following Sunday we drove to the in-laws for coffee, and Willie told his parents of his wonderful investment. Mr. Masterson asked a lot of questions about the location and how much he paid for it, and Willie told him proudly, only $6,000.00. "The elderly farmer just wanted to unload the field. He wasn't concerned about making a profit."

Mr. Masterson reached in his pocket and took out a blank check which he promptly made out for $6,000.00 and passed it to Willie. "Here," he said. "Now the property is mine." Willie said nothing. He took the check and we left for home. I was disgusted and terribly disappointed. Mr. Masterson bullied his son out of a great investment, and built a fancy cottage on the lot we planned on having. I was so upset over this transaction that I wouldn't even visit them there.

That same summer we hosted several card parties and bar-B-Ques at home, and some drinking was involved but not excessive. At least Willie wasn't drinking and driving as much. I was starting to feel like things were gradually working out.

Early one summer evening, one of Willie's distant cousins, Martin Masterson paid him a call. It was a surprise visit as he never contacted us at home before. He arrived at our door with a bottle of whiskey in his hand and a big smile. He knew the liquor was good for an invitation into the house. He was dressed in a navy-blue business suit, white shirt, complete with a blue tie and handkerchief and shiny shoes. He came prepared for business. Willie invited him in and the liquor started flowing smoothly, along with a happy conversation about family and mutual friends. When the bottle was nearly three quarters gone, the real business began.

Martin opened up with, "I've got an opportunity of a lifetime to tell you about. I'm so excited to share this with you! Two other fellows that I trust have joined me in a new venture. They have each put in ten thousand dollars, and so have I. We aren't looking for just a fourth partner in this project, he must be the right person. Someone who will be an asset to the development of this sure to win investment.

We have our sights on a piece of lake front property just outside the city limits that we plan to develop into a picnic and tenting vacation site for middle income families. It's an ideal location, but I can't tell you where it is unless you become part owner. It's all top secret right now, as it isn't even on the real estate market yet, but I assure you, it's a great investment and will bring you returns far greater than ten thousand dollars for years to come. It's going to be my retirement income. This property will be fenced on three sides with lighting for safety. The public will have to purchase passes to enter the grounds and any trouble that arises will be taken care of by the four owners. They will call the police if things get out of hand. We don't anticipate any problems as this tenting area will attract families with children. A staked and fenced portion of the Lake will allow smaller children to play in safety. We plan on a play area with swings and sand boxes and other amusement features. It's endless what attractions we can include for the visitors. We will provide a covered shelter with long tables and benches, and facilities for protective fires, and so much more. There will be no permanent cottages. Just tenting will be allowed, in designated areas. I could go on and on about this exciting opportunity, but I think you can see the possibilities . . . you are a successful businessman. You know a good deal when you hear one. That's why I thought of you. I wouldn't hesitate to trust you with this exceptional offer."

Willie was digesting all the compliments as he slurped down another mouthful of whiskey.

I was listening and watching as I casually went about emptying ashtrays and replacing them with clean ones, placing some nuts and other snacks before them, and generally tidying up. I didn't dare interfere in this business proposal. That was one thing Willie would never allow. I didn't know anything about his business world. That's the way he wanted it.

I didn't like the idea that Martin had to get Willie soused before he could make this business offer. Something didn't add up, but I remained silent.

"Well, Willie, can I count you in?" Martin asked as he poured the final ounce of whiskey into Willie's glass.

"I think it's a worthwhile investment, by the sounds of it. I'll think about it and let you know," Willie slurred, then belched a polite "excuse me."

"Unfortunately, I must receive your commitment today as I have other people I will be offering it too. A deal like this it too hot to last very long on the real estate market. I guarantee it will be snapped up in a hurry, so if you are interested, all you must do is simply write me a check for ten thousand dollars, and you're in. It's as easy as that."

"But I'd like to shee this peeshe of poperty first," Willie slurred.

"As I mentioned before, this is a once in a lifetime offer and it won't last. If you want in, you have to act now." He stood as though he was intending to leave.

Willie said, "Wait! Wait! I have to get my check book." He went to his desk and got the check and wrote it out for the amount required. He passed it to Martin. "Now, tell me where this land is. I'm in now, so let's hear the good news."

"I'll do better than that. I will pick up the other two investors, and we'll all go together to do the finalizing of the deal. I don't have a receipt with me right now, but I'll put one in the mail as soon as I get home. I'll call and let you know when the meeting will take place. It will be soon. I must run now. I hadn't planned on staying this long, but it was great doing business with you, and seeing you again, and getting caught up on all the family news." He left in a hurry.

After Martin left, I said to Willie, "Do you think it was wise to let him leave without a receipt or contract?"

"I know what I'm doing! I don't need you to stick your nose in my business . . . and don't you breathe a word of this to Dad. I don't want him asking for a share of this deal." He left the room to relax and dream of his wonderful investment . . . that never matured.

That was the last we saw of Martin, or the money. He disappeared, to never be heard of again.

***

I decided the house needed painting, inside and out. I was quite good on a paint brush . . . almost as good as on a hoe, shovel, axe or saw. I painted the interior and was well pleased with the results. The outside was a much harder project to tackle, so I got an estimate. The numbers floored me! The best estimate I got was four thousand dollars and they supplied the paint. That covered the stucco plus the trim on the house, the car port, garage, and fence, which was constructed of full sheets of plywood. When I presented the estimates to Willie he had a conniption. He refused to pay that ridiculous price, and had no intention of doing it himself. I let him fume for a while and when I thought his blood pressure had dropped back to normal, I made a proposal. "Willie, if you purchase all the paint, supply the brushes and the turpentine for cleaning the brushes, I'll do the job for one hundred dollars. The deal was made, and I set to work.

Painting the stucco was the most fun. Stucco is rough and it splattered more paint on me than on the walls, but the finished job was beautiful. It was water based paint, so I cleaned up as good as new.

Next was the trim on the house. There was siding across the front, and this took two coats as the wood was extremely dry. I chose a beautiful shade of violet, much to the compliments and complaints of all the spectators and family advisers. Willie was color blind, so he could care less what color I painted the premises.

"Great job Jessie," one neighbor called out. "I wish my wife would paint our house. No such luck. I wouldn't even dare ask." The neighbor ladies avoided me that summer, but I was too busy to care.

I painted the garage and carport with two coats of paint, then started on the fence. The plywood drank the paint like a thirsty camel. I ended up putting on four coats. The job was finally finished and I was pleased with the end results. Willie happily passed over one hundred dollars for my work.

Happiness in my world never seemed to last long. Two weeks later we had a heavy rainstorm and it washed all the paint off my project. Willie got bargain paint, and heaven knows what it was made of. Only the white stucco paint remained intact. For once Willie felt sorry for me. He went after the paint company and they replaced the paint, but not the labor. They said if we had hired professional painters they would have provided painters to redo the job, but because little old Jessie housewife did the work, it didn't count. Well, it takes more than elbow grease and a few gallons of paint to discourage me. I painted it all again, for free.

I didn't realize I was contributing to Willie's drinking problem. I was his leaning post and door mat. He could count on me to do everything pertaining to the house, the children, repairs, juggling the bills, and whatever came along. He took no responsibility of home, marriage or raising the family. I was always available to pick up the pieces, and he knew it.

I must admit, I worked hard on the painting, but satisfaction of a job well done was enough for me, plus one hundred dollars that I could spend any way I wished. That night I looked forward to a peaceful night's sleep.

At 4:00 a.m. the phone rang. Groggy-eyed, I answered, and a female voice said, "Who are you trying to impress?"

I didn't answer for a second or two, as I was half asleep. "Who's calling," I inquired.

"You wouldn't want to know, honey. I've been watching you for a long time," and she hung up.

Chills ran down my spine. It was enough to spoil anyone's dream. It certainly did mine. I lay awake staring at the ceiling till the alarm rang to tell me it was time to start a new day. I mentioned the mysterious phone call to Willie over breakfast and he just shrugged his shoulders and said nothing.

"I wonder who would call and say a thing like that, to anyone at 4:00 a.m." I complained.

"How the hell would I know!" was his answer, and he promptly got up and went to work.

The next night, and for dozens of nights after that, I received a 4:00 a.m. phone call. Sometimes it was just heavy breathing. Sometimes they would hang up as soon as I answered. Then the caller got braver. She'd tell me what I had done that day, or what my kids were doing or wearing. She even told me my son played hockey and got a goal last night. Chills ran up and down my spine. It's one thing to have someone watching old Jessie, but it's a horse of another color when it comes to my kids. She was scaring me. I didn't let my kids out of my sight. I should have notified the police, but I didn't. I had a gut instinct that Willie knew who was making these midnight calls, so I just played along with them, to see how brave they would get.

Finally, after several weeks of this nonsense, the female got up the nerve to really tell me what she wanted. She wanted my husband. "Why don't you let Willie go," she said. "He doesn't love you. He loves me. You could make it a lot easier on everyone if you would just get out."

I took a deep breath, then said calmly, "You know Deary, I would gladly get out and turn Willie over to you, if I thought you were the right person for him. But three other women are calling me off and on and telling me Willie loves them. Now I wouldn't want him to end up with the wrong woman, so I'm taking applications. What are your qualifications?" She hung up and the four o'clock phone calls stopped.

My heartaches didn't stop there. Three other women phoned and said they were pregnant by Willie. I wondered how he found time to work. I did a bit of research and found these women worked in his office. He probably flirted with them and they took him seriously. More phone calls came at odd hours and now I was becoming concerned about my marriage. I took the liberty to search Willie's pockets, and found a phone number on a small piece of crumpled paper, with no name on it. In desperation, I searched the telephone book. This was a task that took a lot of patience, but I was lucky. She wasn't under the letter 'Z'. It was under the name of 'C'. Now I connected the dots, and knew the name of the person making the late evening calls. She was one of Willie's employees. The next time I received an unwelcome phone call that hung up as soon as I answered, I phoned her number. When she answered, I hung up the receiver. This must have touched a nerve, because she phoned back and let it ring three times and hung up before I answered. I phoned back and let it ring three times and hung up. There was a three-minute silence. She phoned back and let it ring twice and hung up, and I did the same. The mysterious phone calls stopped.

Willie came home plastered to the gills, for no reason I knew of, and started picking on me. Maybe his fan club cornered him. Whatever the reason, he had me pinned against the wall and was screaming in my face, telling me how stupid I was. "STUPID, STUPID, STUPID!" he shouted. Billy was a big boy now, and stepped in to protect his mother, and the fight was on. Next,

Sandy got in a few punches and so did I. Willie grabbed Billy's throat and was choking him. I freaked out. I grabbed a broom and shoved the handle into his private property. I guess I was damaging the family jewels, because he let go of Billy and grabbed the broomstick and broke it in half. Anger and liquor gave him the abnormal power to be able to break that broom handle. Billy grabbed his wrists and held them while Sandy was doing her best to get a few punches in. I ran to the phone and called 911. The police were there within minutes and removed us from the house. I didn't know the law. I should have said, "arrest this man," then Willie would have been removed, not the children and me.

I got the best lawyer in town to take care of things for me. I could go back home and remove anything I needed. One big issue was the dog. Our beautiful Samoyed dog was caught in the middle of this mess. We all loved Nicki dearly, but we had no choice. We had to find him a new home. That was easy as Nicki was such a kind, lovable bundle of fur. He went to a country home where there were three children to play with, and a huge field to run in and enjoy. He was happy there, but it broke our hearts to let him go.

Willie made one last attempt to save our marriage, and asked me if I would take him back and make a new start. I said I was willing to try, if he promised to give up drinking. He said he couldn't do that, so I turned and walked away.

I rented a lovely two-bedroom apartment, four blocks away and furnished it with articles from the house. I filed for divorce and our house was put up for sale. I loved my house, but there was no happiness inside. Liquor was causing Willie to become a mental concern. I had to let go and get out before a real tragedy happened. Then I had to forgive Willie for his obvious addiction, and myself, for all the things I did wrong. I had to forgive everyone who hurt me in the past, and start a new life with a clear conscience.

**

The next blow to my world was, my mother died. Over the twenty-three years of my married life, my father, all my siblings and their spouses, passed away. Losing mother was the last straw. There was no one to turn to now. I was at the end of my rope and didn't know which way to turn, so I walked into the Manitoba General Hospital and admitted myself. I was a nervous wreck. I needed help before I had a complete nervous breakdown. At the hospital, I could distance myself from the problem for a time, and I was safe. No one, except my children, knew where I was. It was sad watching people coloring in books and making pussy-tails and playing with dolls. I ended up caring for them and helping them with their projects. This helped to take my mind off my troubles. I was there a week when my best friend found out where I was, and came to rescue me. I stayed with her for a few months, and with doctor's care and a pile of pills, I got myself together. I got a job, started a new life, and I didn't see Willie again for fourteen long lonely years.

I received eleven thousand dollars from the sale of the home, as my share. The house wasn't paid for and it could have been, but Willie's father advised him to keep the mortgage, as the money in the bank was making more interest than he was paying out. He did everything his father told him to do. With my share of the home, I bought a small cottage three blocks from the Lake for four thousand dollars and put a deposit on an older style duplex in downtown Winnipeg. The upper half of the duplex was rented out and the income would help pay the mortgage. Both children were with me all the way. We needed a place to call home.

The day I was supposed to move into my newly purchased home, I found the renter had not moved out, and didn't plan to. He managed to get the rental company to renew his lease for another year, which he proudly produced. I had given notice to my landlord and I would be moving out on the first of the month, which left me with nowhere to go. I went to a lawyer to file a complaint, but soon found the lawyer I chose was the same one the rental management company used. They weren't working for me. They were working against me and I was paying them to do it. Oh, how I needed someone to help me with business transactions. I needed someone I could rely on to guide and instruct me. I needed the sober side of Willie. He would know what to do. All I had were my two lovable children, and my wits. After shedding a few tears, I pulled myself together and gave it some serious thought. What was happening was not my fault. "Someone is to blame and I'm going to get to the bottom of this, and they are going to straighten out this mess," I told the children, with a fraction of uncertainty. I reviewed it out loud. "The house was up for sale. I was told it was empty and it wasn't. The real estate company sold it to me under false pretenses. I'll contact them first."

Naturally the real estate firm wanted to pass the buck. They told me to contact the Trust Company who oversaw the rentals. They were the ones that listed the house for sale. Now I was getting somewhere. I was going to talk to the big boys. I phoned and asked for the name of the President of the A-111 Trust Company of Canada. I was given a name, so I asked to speak to him. The operator asked who was calling, and the nature of my call.

"I'm calling to complain about an error your firm made that has put me and my children out on the street. Don't tell me he is busy. The president of your firm will talk to me, or I will go to the radio stations and the press. I'll pitch my tent in front of your fancy building, where I shall remain until this problem is solved to my satisfaction."

The operator went silent for a few minutes, then said soberly, "Hold the line please."

Patiently I waited. Minutes went by, then a gentleman came to the phone and identified himself as the president of the Trust Co. "I understand you have a concern. How can I help you?"

"That's easy," I replied. "Get the man out of the house you sold me as unoccupied, so I can move in with my family and my belongings. We are presently parked in front of the house with a truckload of belongings and we can't get in. This is something you must take care of immediately, as we have no place to go. I'm willing to set up a tent in front of your place of business until you can straighten this mess out."

"We wouldn't want you to do that, Mrs. Masterson. Give me a little time to sort out the problem and I will get back to you. Just leave it with me."

"Where do I reside while you figure out what to do?" I asked.

"If all else fails, we will put you up in a hotel. I just need a bit of time to get to the bottom of this."

"You have till 6:00 p.m. tonight to solve this problem. Then I will be forced to set up my tent."

"Mrs. Masterson, I quite understand your concern, but you have to give me time to solve this unfortunate misunderstanding, but I promise you I'll do everything I can to have you in your home by midnight tonight."

"I'll call you back in 4 hours and I hope you have some answers."

When I called back the president had good news for me. His firm paid the renter to move out so we could move in. I was to get into my home at last.

"I hope this matter has been handled to your satisfaction, and don't hesitate to let me know if there is anything else I can do for you," the president added.

"Yes, you can oblige me by sending over a cleaning company to wash all the walls, floors, light and bathroom fixtures and vacuum and shampoo the carpets. I want you to remove any garbage created by the cleanup. This will compensate for my stress and discomfort."

I was surprised when he agreed to my demands.

A great load was lifted from my mind. My family would have a home after all.

We happily arrived at the door and were told that the home was still his, as per the lease, until midnight. We were forced to sit in our car and truck, loaded with our every possession and wait until midnight. We had no other option. At the stroke of twelve the young male renter walked out and let us in. He had previously removed all his belongings and just sat out the time till midnight to cause us as much discomfort as possible. He went upstairs to share accommodations with the renter in the upper half of the house. We got everything inside, set up beds to sleep on, and settled down for the night. Tomorrow we would unpack.

Then it started. Loud music was piped in through the heat registers. There was no peaceful sleep allotted to us. Every night thereafter, the music was piped in at 10:00 p.m. and continued until the wee hours of the morning. I confronted the men about the noise and they denied doing anything illegal. I called the police several times but just moments before the police arrived, they shut the music off. They said the music was never on, and that I was a crazy lady.

Billy moved to the basement where it was quieter, and Sandy and I slept with ear plugs on.

We went to our cottage after work on Friday nights and came to work directly from the beach on Monday Mornings. This cut down on our sleep deprivation.

Rent was overdue by three days, so I bravely went to ask for payment. My tenant, Mr. Blackhart, opened the door with a rifle in his hand and it was pointed at me. It was a little unnerving, but I stood my ground and pretended not to notice the gun was pointed at my heart. He passed me the check and I left his premises on shaky legs.

A week went by with the regular loud music piped in. We were trying to ignore the aggravation to not give them any satisfaction. Friday came and we left for the beach as usual. It was a long weekend, and when we arrived back home, we found the house was flooded. Our tenants weren't home, and they had left the water running in the bathtub with the plug left in. All the wiring was soaked in the house. We had no electricity for over a week while it dried out. Then they complained to the rental board that we didn't supply heat or electricity. For this reason, they felt they shouldn't have to pay this month's rent. They had a real game going. After explaining the renter's part in the damages, the rental board took my side. It was considered "accidental." They paid their rent.

Mornings were always hectic getting ready for work. Breakfast was over and lunches made for all of us. I walked quickly to the back door to go to my car but the door wouldn't open. Something seemed to be blocking it. Mystified, I decided to go out the front door and walk around the back of the house where my car was parked, to see what the problem was. Mr. Blackhart had parked his car up against my back door, that's why I couldn't open it. I didn't acknowledge this trick, and went to work. I warned the children to ignore it too.

The next morning the car was gone from the back door, but was parked on my front lawn. I called the police and they told me there was no law against parking on the front lawn. The only law was, you couldn't drive over the sidewalk, but no one saw him drive over it, so there was nothing they could do. Mr. Blackhart knew the law and placed plywood down to drive back to the street.

Rent was overdue again.

Billy was a big fellow, over six feet tall. He had several friends that were equally as big as he was. Billy and three of his biggest friends went to Mr. Blackhart's door and pounded hard, aiming to be heard. When Mr. Blackhart opened the door, the boys were standing in a challenging pose. When they asked for the rent, they received it immediately. There was no loud music that night. The bullies had met their Waterloo.

I decided I was not cut out for being a landlady. I was too young and too timid. I put the house up for sale.

It was Saturday morning and I was busy vacuuming when I heard someone at the front door. There was a small glass window in the door and a face was pressed against it, peering in. His face was covered with an abundance of scraggly gray hair and he looked dirty and scary to me. I didn't open the door. "What do you want?" I shouted.

"I want to purchase your house," he replied, as he stepped back from the window.

I looked the fellow up and down. He looked like a transient. He was poorly dressed and appeared penniless. "Contact the real estate agent," I said, and went back to vacuuming. This was the fellow who purchased my house.

***

Billy finished University with honors and I was the proudest mother in the world. Mrs. Masterson senior said, "Billy should be out working and earning his keep. He doesn't need a University degree. It's a waste of time. He's just going to be in the fish business. There's no need to waste money on useless education."

"My son is going to be educated, no matter what he becomes," I stated firmly. "He may end up being a sewer digger, but he will be an educated one."

Whenever Billy was asked what he was going to be when he finished University he always said, 'an educated sewer digger,' but he ended up being an educated pilot, a successful wine maker, a gentleman and a wonderful son.

Both children decided to rent their own apartments and I moved permanently to the beach and commuted back and forth from there to work. It was the best thing I'd ever done for my peace of mind. The beach was beautiful, even in the winter. Driving home with the moonlight on the snow was romantic and soothing to the soul. I strung Christmas lights all around my cottage and in most of the trees, so it was well lit up when I arrived home in the dark of winter. It was a 50-mile highway drive with little traffic. Who could ask for more? Well, it was lonely but peaceful and my nerves were almost back to normal.

I worked for a small firm as a girl Friday. It was a one girl office, and I was the one girl. Customers came and went and I did everything from sales to bookkeeping, payroll, telephone operator and everything in between. It was a good paying job and I enjoyed the people I worked for.

My car was ten years old and starting to need repairs. I couldn't trust it for highway driving any longer, so I moved back into the city. It broke down often and was causing me a lot of expense and anxiety. First it was the alternator, then it was the regulator, then the alternator, then the regulator, and then the battery, and on and on went the cycle. I couldn't afford a new car and paying the repairs was stripping me financially. I had to find another job to help pay the bills. I worked my first job from 8:00 a.m. to 4:00 p.m. and my second job from 4:15 p.m.to 12:15 a.m. It was a long day. In winter, I would often have to shovel my way out in the morning and my way in at night, in both places.

One morning, I noticed a young boy, about twelve years of age, shoveling his driveway, across the street from my apartment. I stopped and asked him if he would like a job shoveling my parking spot every time it snowed. I offered him two dollars for each time he did the work. He was to do it without asking and come to my suite for pay on Saturdays. He was thrilled with the opportunity to make money. I was thrilled not to have to shovel snow after midnight.

We had a heavy fall of snow, and roads were a mess. I had to shovel my way in and out at my first job and into my second, then out again after midnight. I was looking forward to my clean parking spot when I got home. Upon arrival, I found someone had parked in my nicely cleared space. I had to wake up the apartment manager to have the car removed. More snow fell the next day and when I came home, the same car was parked in my space again. Now I was angry. I Tee parked at the back of his car, and went home to bed. Early the following morning a BANG, BANG, BANG woke me from a sound sleep. The parking space thief couldn't get out and he was stinking drunk and viciously angry. I opened the door and he was so violent I was afraid to tackle him with my words of wisdom. I moved the car and let him out. He didn't park there again.

I worked two jobs for a year and a half, got out of debt and vowed never to let myself fall that low again, and I never have.

At my day job, I got to know the customers well, and we chatted in a friendly manner as their orders were being prepared. Mr. Rob Cruckshank was a regular customer, and he was full of complaints this day. After my car problems and my parking problems, I thought I could match his, and told him so. "What does your husband say about all these problems?" he asked. I thought nothing of the question, and told him I lived alone. He made no further comment and left with his order.

Several days later Mr. Rob Cruckshank came for more supplies and we chatted again, as usual. Before he left, he asked me to join him for dinner. "I'm not trying to hit on you," he said. "I just hate eating alone, and you must feel the same. All I'm asking, is your company, no strings attached. I can either pick you up at your home or meet you at the restaurant, whichever you feel more comfortable with."

It sounded innocent enough, and I accepted his invitation. I met him at a nearby restaurant. It was summertime and the evenings were long and beautiful, so I was in no hurry to leave and neither was he. We both talked up a storm. He told me all about his company that he started in his home, and how it had developed into a huge business and that he was having difficulty handling it alone. He would have to hire someone soon, to do the books and take telephone orders, or make deliveries.

I was careful what information I divulged, but conversation flowed easy and I'm sure more personal details slipped out than I realized. We called it an evening around 8:00 p.m. and I headed home in high spirit.

I hadn't gone far when a car approached me from behind. I saw it coming, at a normal speed and I thought nothing of it, until it hit me. I wasn't wearing a seat belt, and my head hit the rear-view mirror and knocked me out. My car kept going and rolled over the boulevard that separated the four-lane traffic on Portage Ave, and into oncoming traffic. By this time, the car was moving slowly but it rammed head on into a car driven by an elderly couple. I was out cold, laying across the front seat. I could hear voices, but I wasn't responding. People were yelling and pounding on the windows, telling me to pull the button and unlock the door. I slowly sat up and looked at all the faces motioning to me. It wasn't making much sense, but all these young people seemed concerned, so I unlocked the door. Two young men grabbed me, one on each side and forced me to walk . . . it was more like running. They took me across the boulevard to the other side of the street and hustled me along about a block. My feet were hardly touching the ground. We came to a gathering of people, and among them were several police officers and a large group of Hell's Angels. The young fellows turned me over to the police. By now I was coherent.

The driver of the car was a sixteen-year-old girl who didn't have a license to drive. She took her uncle's car without permission and drove it to the pub where she got totally intoxicated. She could hardly stand on two feet, and the Hell's Angels tried to prevent her from driving, but she fought them like a wild cat and managed to get away from them. They followed her to make sure she reached her destination. She fell asleep at the wheel and her foot pushed down on the gas pedal, and that's when she picked up speed and plowed into my car. When she struck my vehicle, she woke up and realized she was in trouble and drove off, but the Hell's Angels followed her and cut her off at the first stoplight. They held her until the police arrived. They gave their statement to the police and I was cleared of all blame, but was without a vehicle. My car was a total write-off. I asked the police to phone Billy to come for me, and he did.

I felt sorry for the old couple I had smashed into. They had just purchased their new car that night and were driving it home from the dealership when the accident happened.

I wasn't hurt badly, just a gash on my forehead. My insurance covered uninsured drivers and they supplied me with a vehicle till my claim came through. My car was a 1966 Strata Chief with little value, so my replacement car wasn't any better.

The next time Mr. Rob Cruckshank came to my office, I told him about my experience. He was understanding and sympathetic. It was nice to share my troubles with someone, as I was feeling all alone against the world.

"You've had quite an experience," he said. "Let me take you out to a movie and dinner. You need to relax."

By this time, I was starting to trust this new-found friend. I allowed him to pick me up at my apartment. The movie and dinner date was enjoyable. Over several cups of after dinner coffees, he asked me to come to work for him.

"I need a secretary like you to help me with my business. Your car is a piece of junk and will start costing you a lot of money for repairs. You'll be right back where you were with the other car . . . a never-ending expense. I will supply you with a company car and pay you one hundred dollars more per month than you are currently receiving. That will help you get back on your feet, financially."

Wow! It sounded too good to be true. He wasn't drunk, and I had never seen him drink or smoke. This made me trust him more than I should have. I could sure use the extra money and a better vehicle. Winter would be coming along in a few months and I wasn't sure this replacement car could hold up through Winnipeg's extreme weather conditions. I loved my present job and all the people I worked with. It was a tough decision. "Oh, Rob, that sounds wonderful. I shall give it some serious thought."

I lay awake most of the night tossing the offer around and around in my head. Was I crazy to give up the job I loved? Was this a windfall opportunity? Is there a hidden agenda that I'm not seeing? I wish I could ask Willie what to do. The sober Willie would have all the answers, but of course he wasn't in my life any more. I decided not to jump into this offer too quickly.

Weeks went by and Rob didn't show up. When he finally arrived for another order, he approached me once again about working for him. I told him I had decided against it. I was content in my present job. Rob went away downhearted but obviously not beaten. He returned a few days later to ask for another dinner date. This time he poured on the pressure. He needed my help.

"Why don't you get someone from the employment center? There are lots of good secretaries out there looking for work," I suggested.

"That's not the point. I need someone I can trust. I'd have to leave them alone in my house while I make deliveries, and they would be free to do all sorts of damage in my absence. I know enough about you to trust you. I'm even willing to make you a partner in my business. With this statement, he pulled out a contract that looked professionally created, giving me fifty percent of his business. Now I'm uncertain. Why would anyone want to give me half of their business? Once again, I told him I would think about it.

I showed the contract to my boss. He went over it carefully and said, "I'd hate to lose you Jessie, but I couldn't stand in your way of success and happiness. This looks like one heck of a good deal to me. Mr. Cruckshank obviously thinks a great deal of you to make an offer like this. You have been a good employee and friend. I wish you all the best."

I helped train another girl to take my place and moved into my new office two weeks later. At first, he had me taking phone orders, filing, and making a few small deliveries. After a week went by he put me on accounts payable and I could see there were a lot of overdue accounts. I tallied them up and made out checks to cover all outstanding bills that were over ninety days.

I would clear them off first. I gave him all the checks to sign, accompanied with invoices and envelopes. He was to take care of mailing them.

Rob went out on some deliveries and I became curious. With so many outstanding payable, I wondered how his receivables were, and checked the balance sheet. I was shocked to see he was in the red, everywhere, with everything. He was in debt over his head. Now I'm worried. What had I gotten into?

When Rob returned from his daily chores, he said he had a successful day. "Tomorrow, I want you to come to the bank with me so I can put your name on all the accounts. I told the banker that you were my new partner and he is most anxious to meet you. We will arrange it so you will have signing authority. You should have this, seeing you are now half owner in the business and it will relieve me of a lot of work and pressure."

I made no comment, but went into deep thought. I shuffled papers around and made myself look busy till the end of the day. I drove home in a state of tremendous uncertainty. I had a feeling I was in big trouble. I trusted a man who didn't drink, but he had other vices that were just as evil and dangerous. He played his hand well, and I didn't recognize the trap.

The next morning, I phoned in ill, which I was, mentally. I went to see a lawyer. I showed her my signed contract and asked her what she thought of it.

"You are fifty percent owner of this business which you say is running in the red. This means you are fifty percent liable for all his debts. If I were you, I would get out of this as fast as you can."

"How can I get out of this agreement? I have signed it and so has he. It is legal and binding."

"I can't tell you to find his copy of the contract and burn it along with your own, because that would be against the law and I could lose my license to practice. You must figure out a way of getting his copy on your own."

Bless her! She told me in a roundabout way, exactly what to do.

I returned to work the next day and waited patiently for Rob to go out on deliveries or whatever he did when he was gone. I searched all the files and drawers on the main floor and found nothing. I had never been upstairs, so didn't know what I would find up there, but I went up to find out. I had to locate that contract in a hurry. I didn't know how long Rob would be away and I wouldn't want him to catch me rooting around upstairs.

It wasn't long before I found the papers. I phoned a taxi and left the keys to his house and car and a note telling him I quit. At home, I watched the papers burn in the sink, then I curled up on the chesterfield and cried myself to sleep.

Rob phoned, but I refused to talk to him. I simply said, "I did the wrong thing and I'm sorry. This is good-bye, and thanks a lot." I hung up. He must have realized I figured out his scheme, because he never called back.

I applied for a new job and was working again in no time. I was hired by a large food chain and catering company. The front of the building was a delicatessen. The staff had to pass through this area to enter the general office. Back of the office was the catering department. My job was accounting, billing, and collecting from all the customers and dividing the gratuity money equally among the seventeen catering staff members.

Each morning, around 9:00 a.m. four male executives marched into the general office, standing stiff, tall, and important. The staff immediately stood up, facing them, and said, "good morning," bowing slightly. The executive members replied, "good morning," and we could then be seated and go back to work.

I worked here three or four days when one of the managers came to my desk and said, "Jessie, you are a hard worker. I like to see that. We need someone like you around here. I would like to take you to lunch and get to know you better."

I said, "Thank you. You are very kind."

"Then you will have lunch with me?" he said, rather surprised.

"It would be my pleasure," I said innocently.

"Thank you," he said with a smile. I'll let you know when that can be arranged."

I thought nothing of this and continued with my work.

The following day there were blizzard conditions outdoors and some of the staff announced that they were leaving early. I paid no attention. I had work to do. A short time later the boss came by and said to me, "I have to drive my wife home. I'll be back shortly."

I didn't understand why he told me that, but said out loud, "No problem" and continued counting stacks of money that I had strewn all over my desk.

"Shh!" the boss said. "My wife will hear you."

I thought that was a strange thing to say, but kept on working.

Suddenly I realized how quiet my surroundings were. There wasn't a soul in my office area. I opened the door to the catering section, and found it in darkness. No one was there. I checked the front delicatessen, and it was closed. Then I got the message, loud and clear. My boss was coming back, and we would be alone. I grabbed my purse and my snow boots and threw my coat over my arm and ran out the door, leaving it unlocked and money spread all over my desk. I was no dummy . . . perhaps a bit slow, but I saw the writing on the wall. I ran down the icy, snow covered sidewalk in my high heeled shoes, facing snow and strong wind in -25 below zero temperature. My car was parked a half block away, and when I finally reached it, I stopped to put on my coat and boots and got into the car to start the engine and warm up. I was shaking as I drove home, knowing I was unemployed, but also knowing I'd done the right thing.

The next morning, I phoned and spoke to the manager. I told him to send my check in the mail immediately, if he knew what was good for him.

He said, "I thought you agreed to have dinner with me."

"Yes, I did, but I didn't realize you had a hidden agenda."

"Well, it takes two to tango," he said with a chuckle.

"You are right, but I'm sorry, I don't dance!"

I was learning how the real world operated, and I didn't like it.

***

It was bound to happen sooner or later. Billy was tall, dark, and handsome, with a personality plus. Girls flocked around him just like they had his father. He finally found a girl that was right for him.

Shelley was a beautiful blue-eyed blonde, registered nurse. Who could ask for more? She joked a lot and seemed to be always laughing. Billy was proud to show her off to his family and friends. He wasted no time in asking for her hand in marriage, and she seemed happy with the proposal. The wedding date was set.

They had a quiet wedding and a honeymoon in Hawaii. They purchased a condo in Winnipeg south, close to the hospital where she worked, and close to the airport where Billy recently was employed by Blue Sky Air Transportation Ltd. His flights took him out of town a lot. Life seemed perfect for the young couple, until Shelley decided to try drinking and drugs when her husband wasn't home. Billy had seen enough drinking in his growing up years and was not willing to condone this sort of behavior. Quarreling began to tear down the tender bonds of marriage. The last straw was when Shelley told Billy she was pregnant, and it wasn't his. It was a dreadful blow to Billy's ego, but he offered to adopt the child. Shelley went along with this plan till the baby was born, then left Billy for good. He was devastated! He couldn't stand the pain of living in the same city as her, with the possibility of occasionally bumping into her and the child. He applied for a job in Kansas City, USA, and moved away to make a new start.

I wondered why Billy was attracted to Shelley. Was there a familiar feeling that drew them together? Was his father's addiction a familiar feeling that he recognized in this relationship? I asked myself these questions and more, but found no answers. No one knows for sure, but thankfully Billy was an abstainer. It would never be condoned in flying. Billy was lonely and heart-broken, but he dedicated his life to flying and was successful beyond his wildest dreams.

***

I moved on to a good paying job with a large Insurance Company, and made a lot of casual friends. I learned to ski, bowl, curl, and golf, but I was lonely. I tried dating, but that didn't work out. Most of the men were looking for rich widows who could keep them in the lifestyle they were hoping to become accustomed to, or just a one-night stand. I took up ceramics and spent my Saturdays making gifts for everyone in my address book. I spent Sundays in church and joined the choir. I managed to fill my lonely days, and years. I still had Sandy around and we spent many hours together, especially on cross country skiing, that we both loved.

Sandy was my baby girl and I loved her dearly. She was so much a part of me. When she took her summer vacation in Vancouver, B.C. she fell in love with the climate, the parks and gardens and the endless activities. She found a job and settled there for life, leaving me totally lost and alone.

***

I heard from a good source that things weren't working out well in Willie's world. The fish marketing board took over all individual fish companies in the province, buying them out at fair market value. Whitefish boats, yawls, and all types of equipment, along with nets, corks, leads and the big freighter were sold and the money divided equally among the major shareholders, but Willie wasn't one of them. He was simply an employee. Willie was left out on the street to fend for himself. It was a blow to his ego. With no skills, trade, or education to speak of, he only qualified for minimum wage jobs, but he still found enough money for booze.

He went to visit his relatives and so-called friends, but found he wasn't as welcome as he was before. Money talks, but when you don't have any, cold unfriendly silence takes over. People can't be bothered with a penniless pauper. He was forced to move to the poor side of the tracks and his lodging was furnished by donations and yard sales. I've heard 'the higher you fly the harder you fall,' so Willie must have hurt his pride badly with this disastrous fall. He worked most of his life in the bowels of hell, holding on to the dream of owning the fish company down the line, but he ended up with grim reality . . . nothing. However, he managed to survive and buy booze, and time moved on.

Willie visited an old friend one evening in mid November, and they had a jolly good time polishing off a twenty-six-ounce bottle of rye whiskey. Time was boldly reaching the midnight hour, but four-year-old Teddy was still running around the house in his pajamas. Willie decided to take the child out for ice cream before heading home. By this time, the parents had consumed enough liquor to cancel brains, because they allowed Willie to take their son in his car, knowing he had a belly full of booze. Ice cream business had slowed down to practically nothing so most of the establishments closed early. Willie drove around, and around, and around, the streets near his friend's home, but nothing was open. He promised the little fellow ice cream and was determined to fulfill that promise, so he kept searching. Before long, the warmth in the car put Teddy to sleep and in the quiet moments thereafter, Willie fell asleep too. The car went off the road, into a deep ditch and rolled over, leaving Willie hanging upside down, securely locked in his seat belt. As the adult seat belt was too large for a child, Willie decided not to use it, so Teddy was tossed about in the rolling vehicle. He now remained in a silent state of unconsciousness. The horrendous impact of the overturned car woke Willie up, but he was unable to move. Blood was running down his arms, across his face, and into his mouth. Spitting and screaming, he made a desperate attempt to release himself and reach the boy, but to no avail. Fear gripped his senses, as reality seeped into his foggy brain. He feared his little friend was dead, because he wasn't crying. "Dear God, I've killed the little fellow! Heaven help us!" He screamed and screamed for help, hoping someone would miraculously hear his urgent cry. It wasn't long before police arrived on the scene – and an ambulance was called. Two police officers managed to pry the broken door open and shone a light inside, looking for other occupants. Willie screamed for them to cut his seat belt and free his body, but the police ignored him, as they reached in to remove the limp body of a child. The paramedics arrived and took over. Both passengers were removed from the wreck. Willie collapsed on a stretcher and peed his pants. He kept crying and pleading to any ear that would listen, wanting to know if the boy was alive. The accident victims were rushed to the emergency ward at the Manitoba General hospital. Willie had cuts and bruises to his arms, face and head and was bleeding profusely. Nurses and doctors were frantically trying to clean and bandage him, but he fought them with all the strength he had left. He was fraught with fear and wanted to see Teddy. "How is the boy? Is he O.K? Is he alive? Please leave me alone and look after Teddy," he cried. The nurse said she didn't know the condition of the child because he was taken to the children's ward, but she would inquire. At this point, Willie vomited all over himself, further solidifying his popularity with the medical team. They left him to stew with the spoils of the night, and exited the room.

When the nurse returned, Willie was crying pathetically and tearing at his bandages but he calmed down instantly when she told him, "The boy is alive, but will remain in the hospital for a few days for observation. We want to make sure his internal organs are not damaged. He has several cuts, bruises and broken bones but is very much alive. His parents are with him now. You are both lucky to be alive. I hope you have learned a lesson tonight. You should be ashamed of yourself," she added in disgust, and with lack of sympathy, she left the room.

"I will never drink again," he sobbed. "Never, never, never!"

That's what had to happen for Willie Masterson to admit whiskey was a dangerous and destructive element in his life. It was a problem he could master . . . if he wanted to. Alcoholics Anonymous was available, but he was too proud to go that route. All his family were heavy drinkers and thought Willie was hilarious when he acted the fool, and I had always been available to apologize, pick up the pieces, pay the price, whatever the cost, and take him home to sleep off the effects of his happy hours.

***

Sandy met Randy Fitzgibbon, the man of her dreams, and they were planning to get married. She lived in B.C. but wanted to be married in the church of her childhood, the beautiful Westminster United Church in Winnipeg. She phoned one day and said, "Mother, do you think you and Daddy could be civil to each other for one day? I would like you both at my wedding."

I promised to be civil if Willie could promise the same. I had no idea he had given up drinking, and did not know the reason why until much later, and so the wedding plans were made.

Sandy looked stunningly gorgeous in her snow white, floor length wedding gown that was draped with a shimmering veil flowing from a sparkling tiara. It was outshone only by her bright blue eyes and beautiful smile. She carried a cascade of orange tiger lilies to compliment the autumn season.

The bridesmaids and the mother of the bride and the mother of the groom wore peach floor length dresses with corsages of peach rosebuds and soft fern. The men were in chocolate brown tuxedos and were decked out with peach boutonnieres, but it was Colleen, the five-year-old flower girl that stole the show, with her sweet innocence, her long peach colored dress and floral headdress. She carried a tiny basket of peach rosebuds and petals and gently sprinkled them along Sandy's pathway.

It was a traditional wedding with a full course meal, orchestra, wedding cake, and all the little extras, including streamers and decorations. Wedding pictures were taken in the beautiful West Kildonan Park where she loved to go as a child. Speeches were made and the first dance was announced. Then the parents were invited to join in. Willie reached for my hand and wheeled me around on the floor, just like he used to do in the good old days. What a strange sensation flowed over me, and no doubt it affected him as well. He was well dressed and perfectly sober. We hadn't seen each other for fourteen years and it was apparent, the fire had never died out completely. Still I was skeptical. I couldn't help recalling how well he hid his alcoholism from me before we were married. What a shame liquor destroyed a beautiful human being. We had a few more dances before the night was over and then we departed, going our separate ways.

Once again Willie did his research and found where I was working, and the following Monday he phoned me.

"It was nice seeing you again, Jessie. You are looking great. I was just wondering if you would like some pickerel fillets and perhaps some pickerel cheeks. I remember how you used to enjoy them."

"Thanks Willie. It's kind of you to offer. I haven't had pickerel for years, but you needn't worry about that. I will survive without them . . . I have for fourteen years," I said politely.

"Yes, it's been a long time for me, and I regret that it happened, but that was yesterday and yesterday's gone. I am going out of town on business for a few days, but if you would like some pickerel, I'll get some and leave it in my fridge. The key to my apartment will be under the doormat. I don't mind leaving it there because I have nothing anyone would want to steal. Don't be afraid. I won't be there. The fish will be in the fridge for you." He gave me his address and hung up before I had time to thoroughly balance out this equation.

I pondered his offer for a long time, then decided I'd take a chance. He wasn't the type of person who would physically harm me, and he was a perfect gentleman at the wedding . . . and cold sober. He was just like the young man I met at the toboggan slide so many years ago. Sadly, liquor had the power to destroy a lovable, hard working human being and transfer him into a fearfully deranged mortal.

Curiosity made me do it. I drove over to his apartment. It was in the poorer part of town and the building looked like it had been a small warehouse at one time. The wood siding needed painting and repairs. The concrete steps were crumbling to dust in several places. The general appearance spelled poverty. There wasn't a soul around, and not a sound other than traffic noise from the nearby street. I must say it was a bit spooky. Carefully I ventured forth and looked under the well-worn doormat. The key was there. Should I, or should I not, enter this building? I pondered the point for several moments before finding the courage to enter.

The room was spotlessly clean, but practically empty. Everything looked second-hand . . . a rickety wooden table, two old wooden chairs that didn't match, an ancient beat up fridge, a faded chesterfield with lumpy cushions, a single bed with plenty of covers, but nothing fancy. Everything he owned looked like it had been purchased at a flee market. Curiosity made me open the cupboard to see what antiques may be hidden there. I found a well used electric frying pan, one small saucepan, a stack of paper plates, two coffee mugs, one knife, fork and spoon, and a jar of instant coffee. It told a sad story of hitting the bottom of the proverbial pit. It was a far cry from the little rich boy I once knew. It was hard to believe he had once flown so high and now had fallen so low. I choked back a bitter tear.

He hung hand written posters all over the windows, doors, fridge, and chairs. Much to my dismay they all read, "I love you Jessie." This is what he wanted me to see, more than the fish.

I opened the fridge and found very little in the way of food, but a large parcel of fish was there with my name on it. I took it out and was about to make a fast exit, when I noticed a card standing upright on a beat-up wooden box that he used as a night table. I picked it up, and was surprised to find it was one I had given him on Father's Day many years ago, and he had cherished it all those years. I had signed it, "Love, Jessie." A rush of old, familiar, forgotten feelings washed over me. I left in a hurry before I did something stupid.

A few days later, Willie phoned and asked me out for lunch. I felt indebted for all the lovely fillets, and accepted the invitation. "My lunch hour is just one hour, Willie. I'm not an executive yet, so I don't have those two and three-hour lunch breaks. But if we meet some place near my office we should be able to make it. By the way, how can you get the time off?" I asked.

"I'll make up the time by working late tonight," he replied. "I work for an old friend of mine and he does me favors occasionally, as long as the work gets done."

The next day we met at a local Chinese restaurant near my place of employment. Willie arrived with a huge bouquet of red roses. I could tell he had been crying, because his eyes were red and swollen, so how could I not accept them. We had a quick lunch and I thanked him for the fish and the flowers, but told him not to expect too much in return. "I hold a good position with the firm I work for, and I make good money. I am independent now. There's nothing left of the shredded pieces of yesterdays, so please don't try to patch up the broken hearts, the hurts, and home. It won't work. We can be friends, if you wish . . . but that's all."

Willie jumped up and quickly kissed me in front of the world, and we both went our separate ways.

Willie has always been a determined fellow and willing to fight for what he wanted. That part frightened me. I knew I had a battle to face or maybe it was a war. Time would tell.

I was busy at work and grateful for the distractions, but it didn't last forever. Every Monday a bouquet of roses arrived on my desk. I was kidded a lot by my fellow workers and I'm sure I blushed unwillingly. I had to do something, so I spoke to my boss and asked if there was any chance of me being transferred to British Columbia. I told him I wanted to be near my daughter, and that was partially true. He said he would inquire and see what he could do.

A few busy months slid by and Sandy called to inform me she was expecting a baby. I was excited and determined now to move, with or without a transfer, but my boss sensed the urgency in my voice and made the move possible.

The next time Willie phoned for a luncheon date, I told him the good news regarding the up-coming grandchild. I told him I'd be moving at the end of the month. I wished him well and told him I'd keep him posted regarding the baby's arrival. He was delighted he was going to be a grandfather, but made no comment about me moving away. I was pleased about that.

I sold my few belongings and packed what I could in my car and set out for the Rockies. It was a long and scary trip, as I ran into snow when going through the mountain passes, but I made it.

Sandy was happy to see me, and sad at the same time. She welcomed me into her living room, and there I got the shock of my life. Sitting calmly in a big easy chair, was Willie, enjoying a cup of coffee. I nearly fainted. What could I say? He had as much right to be there as I did.

"Well, surprise, surprise!" was all I could muster up to say.

Willie explained quietly. "Sandy needed me, so I borrowed money from my boss and headed here as quickly as I could. My boss arranged for me to work for a friend of his in Richmond . . . I start tomorrow. I had to do a lot of praying that my little bucket of bolts would make it through the mountains. It got me here, but it was dirty and dusty from the travel, so I decided to clean it up before arriving at Sandy's home. When I put it through the car wash, the fender fell off," he said with a jolly laugh. "I'll have to get it fixed. I can't afford a new car right now, and I can't drive it without a fender."

I was speechless.

"I knew you were coming here Jessie, but I also knew you would be working long hours and wouldn't be here for Sandy all the time, so I'm staying with her till she has her baby. She is not doing well and needs me. Her husband is not doing his duty, I'm sad to say."

I drove over 1500 miles to get away from Willie, and here he was as large as life. It's hard to believe he came to help his daughter. He did nothing to help with the kids when they were growing up. Well . . . maybe he has grown up. I'll watch for the signs. I hope they don't blow me away. I gritted my teeth, then put my hand over my mouth to prevent me from blasting him with a lifetime of painful hurts and regrets. Like, where was he when I was pregnant and suffering from morning sickness? Where was he when I was frightened? Where was he when the kids were hurt or ill? Where was he when I needed him? Now he's here, showing up like a hero, to help his daughter. I was not impressed.

As it turned out, he was a blessing. Sandy was in and out of emergency every two or three weeks. She couldn't seem to hold food down and was extremely thin. When she vomited during the night her husband just rolled over and covered his head with his pillow so he couldn't hear her. He constantly complained that she was disturbing his sleep. At the same time, Sandy was trying to work full time. She needed her job as Randy was a poor provider, but a good eater.

I found lodging close to my work and equally close to Sandy's house. I had all the comforts of home, but I was worried about my darling daughter.

The months were long and stressful for everyone, but finally a beautiful little boy came into our world. He was lying undressed on his blanket, waiting for the nurse to put on a dry diaper, and I leaned over to give him my most proud and welcoming smile, when he peed in my face and down the front of my blouse. That part of him was in good working order. The nurse laughed and so did everyone else. She said, "That's good luck, Grandma. It means you and this child have a permanent bonding for life. You have just been christened."

The baby was perfect and mother was doing well. She was home in three days. However, baby Kevin had the colic and cried off and on all night. That was the last straw for Randy. He packed his duds and left. Now Sandy, Grandpa and Grandma had a full-time job. Everyone had to work, and it took a lot of juggling to cover all bases. Eventually, a day care became a necessity and life gradually became routine.

Every Saturday Willie picked me up and we went garage sale shopping for Kevin. Clothing was cheap as were toys, highchairs, walkers, swings, and playpens. We made sure he had everything he needed, and more. What we couldn't find at garage sales, we shopped for later, in local stores. We both lived and breathed for Kevin. He brought us all the joy our hearts could hold. He was beautiful. We spent every minute we could, giving him loving support and most of all the feeling of security.

Willie was doing well at his job, and purchased a second-hand truck. Then he bought a run-down house, and in his spare time he cleaned it up, painted and repaired it, put in new carpeting, washed the windows, raked the yard, and made it look decent. Then he sold it at a nice profit and bought another one. This got him on his feet financially.

Every Friday he met me after work with a bouquet of flowers and took me out to a nice restaurant for dinner. Saturday morning was garage sale shopping, then in the evening we went dancing. I loved the dance music, and the exercise was good for me, as I sat most of the day at work. Sundays, I picked up Sandy, Willie, and the baby, and we went to church. Life was full, happy, active, and rewarding. Willie was the same old sweetheart I met years ago at the toboggan slide. I told myself not to be taken in, that I would only get hurt like before.

***

It was sad to see Sandy alone. She was tall, slim, blonde, and had personality plus. To Willie and me, she was beautiful. When Randy departed, he left her the home, which she paid for anyway, but by law he could have claimed half. He couldn't seem to keep a job, and Sandy had been supporting him, so he wasn't a huge loss. She had a good car and a good job. She was ripe for the picking. It wasn't long before a vulture landed.

Frederick Hammerfield was a handsome chap, in a rugged sort of way. He was a wheeler dealer, fast talker, and the authority on any subject you wished to discuss. He owned a photography shop, a yacht, an expensive new truck and ran a vending machine company. Sandy fell for it all, but Willie and I had our doubts. He was charming and treated Sandy well. They were always going somewhere, and we were called on to babysit often. We didn't mind, as we dearly loved being around Kevin. It was nice to see Sandy happy, and we wished her the very best.

***

As well as working full time, Willie was buying, repairing, and selling homes on a regular basis. Most of the homes only needed cleaning and a few repairs, like painting, re-carpeting, washing windows and cleaning the lawns or hauling garbage to the dump. He made a good profit on these houses and could pay back all the money he borrowed to get started. However, the market was changing. After he sold his last home, he couldn't find another old one in his financial bracket. He had real estate people searching, and he hunted on his own as well. It was getting close to the time to move out and he had nowhere to go. He had no choice, he had to move back into Sandy's home till he could get another fixer-upper. Nothing was coming his way. The Real Estate market skyrocketed over night and he didn't have the down payment required for any of the homes available. He was stuck. Banks weren't interested in helping him and he was becoming desperate.

The flowers, dating and dancing had gone on for 10 years, and we were good friends. I had to admit that liquor was the whole problem in our past, and that no longer existed. I put a lot of thought into my own future. I was getting older and my hair that once was a beautiful auburn color, was now a glistening white. The money I carefully saved wouldn't pay for a home for me, like I had dreamed it would. A few health problems were showing their ugly heads, and I was concerned about Kevin growing up with a grandma in one end of town and a grandpa in another. Soon he would be asking questions we wouldn't like to answer. I hashed this problem over, and over, and over, again. What would be the best thing to do, for all concerned. I stewed on this for several days. I talked to friends I could trust. No one wanted to commit themselves, and be responsible for my mistakes. It was a decision I had to make.

I looked back on my life – right back to the time I first met Willie. I had nothing. I couldn't even afford to pay for my wedding. I owned three dresses and two pairs of shoes, a coat, substantial underwear and stockings, a bit of Woolworth jewelry, and a job that paid me $19.65 a week. I didn't consider myself poor, or broke, but I was. I just didn't know the difference. Willie knew the difference, and accepted me for what I was, no questions asked. Although he drank up a storm and caused me heaps of heartaches during the twenty-three years of marriage, I never went hungry or without very much of anything. The children were well taken care of and were badly spoiled. How could I see Willie struggling financially right now and not help him? He took me with nothing. Why can't I take him with nothing? I thrashed this problem over for days, then decided to take the plunge.

It was most unusual for me to invite Willie to my apartment, so it must have been quite a surprise when I asked him to stop by. I told him I'd put the coffee on. He probably broke the speed limit coming over, because he was there before the coffee was perked.

"Is something wrong?" he asked with genuine concern.

"Not really," I replied in business fashion. "I have something I'd like to discuss with you. It's just an idea I've come up with. I don't want you to accept my proposal unless you are comfortable with it. Am I understood?"

I poured us both a cup of coffee, then I asked the question, "How much money do you need to purchase the next home you plan to renovate?"

Willie was silent for several moments, his head hung low. Taking a deep breath, he replied in a defeated tone, "probably $30,000.00. The banks won't lend me that much money," he said as he swallowed a sob hidden in the back of his throat. I had plans that will never mature now.

"I wanted to make enough money to pay for a home in full, then maybe you would consider coming back to me, but I guess I've lost you again. I'm sorry Jessie. I still love you, and I still had hope."

I gulped back a tear and said, "I can lend you the money Willie, but we must iron out a few details. I want to make it perfectly clear, I have worked hard to accumulate this money and I don't plan on throwing it away foolishly. I think we can work out a deal where we both profit.

First, I want a say in what you purchase, and where. Whatever money you have, I will match it, and not a penny more. Both names must go on the title. We will both continue to work, and in our spare time we will renovate the home and make it livable, presentable, and attractive for selling purposes. All overhead expenses will be shared equally. Instead of paying rent elsewhere, I shall move in to one of the rooms, so the house must have at least two bedrooms. We will do our own cooking and laundry and live our separate ways, in a businesslike fashion that will profit both of us. We will live under the same roof, but separate. In time, if we find that we can live together again, we can discuss marriage, but common law is out of the question. I feel if I'm good enough to sleep with, I'm good enough to marry. If it doesn't work out, we sell the house and go our separate ways. That's my offer. Take it or leave it. The choice is yours."

Willie was sobbing and shaking like a little boy in an old man's skin. "I'm willing to give it a try, and I'll do my best to make it work, I promise." He jumped up from his chair and flew into my arms, and cried on my shoulder. I was close to crying too.

We met with a real estate agent and told her what we were looking for. "Don't waste your time or mine, showing us something beyond our means. We have leveled with you regarding what we can afford, and we expect the same respect from you. If you fail to abide by our requests we'll find a new agent that will."

Every night after work we viewed a home or two until we found the one that was just what we wanted, and the price was right. It was on a respectable street and had a large yard with fruit trees . . . something I always dreamed of having. There were three large bedrooms, a living room, dining room with a fire place, and a small kitchen. All it needed was some TLC and a lot of elbow grease, and we had plenty of both. We signed the deal and moved in before we had a chance to even clean it properly. We had lived in Majestic point, Seagull Landing, and Critter Creek, to name a few, and the homes there were no fairyland castles. We nestled into our dwelling place and began cleaning up the mess. Willie took four truckloads of garbage to the dump the first day, and that gave us a starting point. I asked for vacation time from work so I could make my bedroom comfortable and clean the kitchen and bathroom to my approval. Willie worked diligently every weekend, from morning till dark. We hardly spoke to each other till the day was over. Then we were too tired to talk. Our minds were dwelling on better days ahead.

***

Sandy came bouncing in the door all excited. "Look Mom! Dad come and see!" She held out her hand to display a beautiful diamond ring. "Frederick asked me to marry him, and I said yes. We are going to be married on his yacht. Isn't that exciting?"

I turned ice cold. Something didn't sound right. They hadn't known each other for long, and I knew from experience that it's not the way to go, but she was so excited, I had to hold her, love her, and wish her the best in the world.

Shopping, planning, and organizing for the wedding went full speed ahead. This took a little time away from the renovation project we were up to our neck in, but our children always came first. This was Sandy's second marriage, so it was a little easier to plan. The yacht couldn't accommodate many people, so that cut the planning down a great deal.

The day of the wedding was sunny and warm and the bride looked gorgeous in her cream colored floor length wedding dress. The groom looked handsome in his brown suit and little Kevin stole the show in his tuxedo. The service was the usual, other than it was in open air and it was difficult to hear, because there was a brisk wind blowing. A full course meal was served and a disk jockey played music for dancing. Once again Mother and Father danced at her wedding. Liquor flowed in abundance, but Willie didn't touch a drop . . . neither did I.

The bathrooms on the yacht were on the lower deck, and I had to use the facility. Somehow, I managed to lock myself inside this tiny cubical, as the yacht was bouncing gently with the waves. With music blaring, no one could hear my screams, or me kicking the door down. Eventually someone else needed to relieve themselves and heard my pitiful pleadings. They tried to open the door from the outside, but it was jammed. The groom was finally called to rescue the unhappy prisoner. He had to remove the hinges to let his brand-new mother-in-law out. Was this prearranged, I wondered? It was the joke of the evening, but it wasn't funny for me as I have a tendency toward claustrophobia.

Frederick had no parents in attendance, just two brothers who downed a few free drinks and left as soon as the boat docked. I must admit, it was a beautiful wedding, simple but elegant.

The happy couple went to Hawaii on a honeymoon and we had Kevin all to ourselves. When the newly weds returned they lived in Sandy's home. They seemed happy, and that's all that mattered. Still I kept my eyes open for something . . . I didn't know what. It was just a feeling. I mentioned my feelings to Willie, but he scolded me for being so negative, so I forced my worrisome thoughts, and my mouth closed.

Sandy continued to work, dropping Kevin off at day care every morning and picking him up in the evening. She cooked and cleaned and served her husband as a dutiful wife. Frederick was always tired when he got home and found the nearest easy chair and a remote control, and a bottle of beer.

The house wasn't paid in full, so the financial subject surfaced. Frederick decided that seeing he made the most money *(he claimed)* he would bank all his wages and they would live on Sandy's. That way they could pay the mortgage off sooner, and eventually have a neat little nest egg for retirement. It made a lot of sense to Sandy, so they opened a 'retirement' bank account and the savings began.

One of the rooms in their home became Frederick's private office. All paperwork was done here and recorded on his computer. Sandy never had the time in her busy life to learn how to operate a computer, nor did her place of employment require her to have this knowledge. Frederick often made snide remarks about her being stupid, and although it hurt her feelings she felt he was just fooling.

***

Each day Willie and I stood back and admired what we had accomplished. It was such a joy to watch this house blossom into a beautiful home. Walls and ceilings were painted, windows washed, new carpeting throughout, ceramic tile on the kitchen and bathroom floors, and new light fixtures. The interior looked great, but needed furniture. That would come with time. We tackled the outside. The roof was in good condition, but we painted the exterior and repaired places that needed attention. We raked the lawn and made gardens, planted flowers and shrubs.

As time passed, we invested in furniture and were the happiest unwed couple on the street. The time had come. Willie proposed once again, and I'm not sure if I wanted to marry Willie or the house. I was in love with the castle we created together.

"If we marry, there will be no drinking," I firmly announced, and Willie promised with all his heart and soul that he would never touch another drop, so plans were made for a quiet dinner party in our beautiful home. We were pleased to show it off to our family and close friends. We were married by the Justice of the Peace, and felt we had patched our broken world back together again. Billy flew home for the happy occasion and it was wonderful to have all the family together.

Life went on smoothly for several years. We couldn't have been happier. We still went dancing every Saturday night and as usual all the ladies flocked around him. What man wouldn't enjoy that? My flower gardens were awesome, so the Friday night floral bouquets stopped arriving. "You don't need my little bouquets anymore, Jessie. You have tons of flowers in your garden." *(Men see things differently)*. I pretended I agreed with him. The family still went to church together every Sunday, all except Frederick. He said he wasn't into that.

***

Our neighborhood was quiet with many vacant lots available. We liked it that way, but it wasn't to last. A huge elaborate looking Casino was constructed two and a half blocks from home. It had several Black Jack tables and five hundred slot machines. It didn't bother me at first, but it soon became a fly in the ointment. Willie was obsessed with it, and that caused me grave concern. He still paid his half of everything so I couldn't complain, but sometimes he would gamble for five to eight hours, nonstop, and he went there every day. I dropped in to see what he was up to, and sat in the seat beside him for over an hour and he didn't know I was there. He was mesmerized by the machines. It was like he was part of them. I walked away to absorb what was really happening. I didn't want to believe it, but it appeared my darling baby blue-eyed Willie gave up one addiction and found another . . . or perhaps it's just something new and exciting and it will wear off in time. I had to give him the benefit of the doubt.

***

Years flew by and Kevin grew to be a handsome lad. Most children his age knew how to operate a computer, as well as other digital equipment, better than their parents. Sandy asked Kevin if he would show her how to use the computer. He was happy to do so, even though he had strict orders from his stepfather to never touch it because it contained valuable information that he would hate to lose.

"First thing you do Mom, is turn it on like this," he instructed. "Then it depends what you want to do. If you want to send a message, you open Outlook, or whatever program is installed on your computer. There are different programs that do the same thing. Let me show you." He opened Frederick's E-mail account and a list of letters appeared from a lot of women Sandy knew. She was mildly surprised. "Can you open that one, Kevin?"

"Sure Mom."

Sandy was shocked at the contents of the letter. It was a personal and sexy love letter from someone she considered a friend. She didn't want to alarm Kevin, but the tears began to blur her vision. Kevin was more than helpful. He showed his mother where to find the sent and deleted messages as well, and how to print them out. She thanked him and sent him out to play while she did some exploring on her own.

It was painful beyond words, but she knew she had a problem that needed attention. She copied all the letters to and from the group of girlfriends her husband was flirting with. This was positive proof of his unfaithfulness. She knew it was more than just a casual flirtation. She placed all her evidence in a folder and tucked it away safely. Then she paid a visit to the bank. The retirement account had a balance of $155.32. Where was all the money he was supposed to be depositing? Had he placed all the money on the mortgage? She inquired and found that wasn't the case. Did he have an account in Switzerland, or was he having a royal ball at her expense? There was only one way of knowing for sure. She would have to confront her lover-boy husband.

"I went to the bank today Frederick, to see how our savings account was coming along. I was hoping I could retire soon, and I got quite a surprise. "Where is all the money you promised to save for our retirement?" she asked.

"I don't know what you are talking about, Sandy darling! I don't recall any arrangement made between us. My money is my money, and your money is your money. What you spend your money on is your business, and the same goes for me."

"Don't you dare call me 'Sandy darling', you rotten thief. You have sponged on me for ten years, and I trusted you with all my heart, but you aren't getting away with this. I'm seeing a lawyer and you had better have some good answers for what you have done with your money."

Frederick laughed and went to his office to get his recent e-mails.

Sandy met with a lawyer who advised her that there was nothing much she could do, other than get a divorce. The money could not be recovered, but he could try putting a lien against Frederick's businesses for his board and room for the past ten years and see what the judge will allow. It's worth a try, but there's no guarantee.

It went to court and the judge was lenient because of all the letters from girlfriends, and the fact that he paid nothing for his keep in the past. He ordered the house to be sold and the money split in half, plus Frederick had to pay $70,000.00 for his upkeep for the past ten years.

Sandy was sad it came to this, but moved on to a better life with her little son at her side. She purchased a house with a big yard for the boy to play in. It was close to a school and to her work. Willie and I were always there for her, but we wished we could wipe the sadness from her eyes.

***

Willie slipped off to the casino every chance he could. If I happened to sleep in any morning, I would find him missing from the household when I awoke. He left no message, but I knew exactly where he was. When he came home he always said he made a few dollars or broke even. I could easily tell the truth. If he won, he was a happy fellow. If he lost, he was cranky in proportion to the amount he donated to the slot machines. If the loss was substantial, Willie became a bear and shouted at me for the least little thing. If I asked a simple question he wouldn't answer or he'd shout, "How the hell do I know!" This became his favorite vocabulary these troublesome days.

There were times when I thought money was missing from my purse, but I had no proof. It kept happening, so I set a trap. I put a tiny drop of nail polish on the corner of all my bills. One such bill ended up in Willie's possession and that proved to me he was stealing from me when he ran short of gambling money. I decided to say nothing, but kept my finances hidden or close at hand.

Our financial arrangement was on a fifty-fifty basis from day one of our reunion. I took care of paying the mortgage payments, utility bills, medical, insurance and taxes. These came automatically out of my bank account, and on the first of each month Willie paid me his fifty percent. Other miscellaneous expenses were equally paid as they arrived, along with the groceries bills. This system worked smoothly, prior to the arrival of the casino in our lives. Now it was becoming a bone of contention. The first of the month became the third, fifth or fifteenth, or whenever I could catch up with him. Each time he paid his dues, there was a quarrel. I had to provide proof of payment for all the above, and then he would reluctantly pay his share. This was putting a dreadful strain on our relationship.

Willie started complaining about everything, especially my cooking. This was a touchy subject because I was never taught to cook, and with Willie being away from home a great deal in the early years of our marriage, I had no reason to create fancy meals, but as time went by I learned to put a decent meal together. It was far from gourmet, but was healthy and plentiful and no one ever went hungry.

Then the hammer of life came crashing down. Willie lost his job. He was sixty-three, with no education and very little skill or experience in anything. Unemployment provided a small amount of money for a short time and he applied for early Canada pension. The easy money coming in, and all the free hours, allowed Willie to live at the casino every day. He managed to come home in time to make supper for me, which I appreciated. He kept the house clean and did the laundry and became the official stay at home Dad.

One day I came home from work and Willie wasn't there. It was a strange feeling to witness the silence, dinner not ready, and the breakfast dishes still in the sink. I didn't know what to make of it, but started cleaning things up and preparing something for us to eat. About 7:00 p.m. Willie arrived. He came home because he had no other choice. He stood inside the doorway and danced up and down like a child wetting his pants, and cried, "I lost it all! I lost all my money! I was sure the slot machine would eventually cough up a big pile and I'd give it all to you. It just didn't happen for me. I'm sorry. I won't be able to pay my share of expenses this month, but I'll make it up to you next payday. Honest I will."

He kept on dancing nervously up and down, and the look on his face was pathetic. Poor old Willie lost again, and he expected me to feel sorry. I felt nothing!

I agreed to bail him out this time, but made him understand that I would never do it again. He cried like a baby and gave me a big hug and a sloppy tear-stained kiss.

The next monthly payment came due and I demanded my check on the 1st of the month. He was very indignant. "I paid you three days ago. Now you are trying to cheat me," he screamed in anger.

"What do you mean you paid me? You most certainly did not!"

"Oh, yes I did, and I can prove it." He pulled out his check book and showed me the carbon copy of a check made out to me for the total amount owing. It was dated three days prior. I couldn't believe my eyes. It looked legitimate, but I did not receive this check. Still I was puzzled. He had the carbon copy as proof. Something was wrong here. I picked up my purse and walked out the door. I went to the bank and asked for a printout of my account. Just as I expected, that money was not there. I explained my dilemma to the clerk and she casually stated, "Unless your husband wrote the check out and destroyed it . . . then he would still have a carbon copy."

The light bulb went on in my mind. What a clever trick . . . and he almost got away with it. I thanked the clerk and left. I sat in the car and cried my heart out. My husband was smitten with a terrible disease, gambling! His alcoholism was replaced by another obsession that was crippling his mind and his financial future. I knew this was the end of the rope.

Our home was two years from being paid in full, but the stress of carrying the financial burden was too much to ask of me. I could have slapped his wrist and bailed Willie out one more time, but what guarantee was there he wouldn't do this again . . . and again.

I collected my thoughts, then faced Willie and the problem. "We must sell our beautiful dream home, split the money and go our separate ways. Thanks Willie, for a few years of true happiness. We were on the top of the mountain, and now we are at the bottom of the slippery slope, just like when we first met. We are at the point where we have to roll over and get off the track to avoid a crash, dust ourselves off and walk away."

Willie was unhappy about the breakup because he needed a cook and someone to cater to his personal needs, but the selfish side of him was excited to receive his share of the money from the sale of the house. Now he could have a ball at the casino with all that money to play with. I'm sure he had dreams of beautiful young ladies chasing him, like in his younger days as well.

Neither of us was shedding a tear. The river of regrets had finally dried up. I was emotionally drained but not willing to try another round of broken dreams.

I learned that addictions are a dreadful disease of excuses, but they can be cured if the person is willing, but often one obsession is simply replaced by another. Liquor, infidelity, gambling, cheating, habitual lying, and drugs, can destroy whoever chooses to slide down the hills of temptation, and destroy innocent people they happen to drag with them, on the slippery slopes of reality.

Where Willie moved to, I'll never know. I don't want to know. He was my one and only love and I know it wouldn't take much to fan the flames if I saw his sad baby blue eyes again. Just one pleading look and I'd be a goner. Before that happens, I must turn over a new page in my book of life.

I, Jessie McGann Masterson, retired from my long-standing employment and moved into a beautiful assisted living place and started a new life. I made many new and understanding friends.

I was sitting alone in the far-off corner of the lunch room thinking of the past years, the ups and downs a person goes through looking for love, peace and understanding . . . things money can't buy. I thought Willie was a good man, but the poor fellow had an illness he couldn't control. Compulsive addictions are cancers that constantly consume its victim. When Willie refrained from drinking and gambling, there wasn't a nicer person on the face of the earth, but when he became a victim of his obsessions, he wore the devil's crown.

Forgetting the past won't be an easy task, but after all I've been through in life, I know I can adjust to almost anything. Deep down in my heart there remains a tiny spark of hope for the future. I'm sure there's happiness for me somewhere . . . somewhere beyond the blue horizon.

EPILOGUE

Her thoughts were far away in another time and place, so she didn't see the gentleman who quietly seated himself beside her, until he spoke.

"Hello, Jessie," he said. "How nice to see you again."

She gazed into the smiling face of a well-dressed gentleman, who was cleanly shaven, had a heavy crop of snow white hair, sparkling white teeth and a complexion as clear as a new born baby's bottom.

"You don't remember me, do you?" He said with a grin. "Well, I could never forget you. I had a crush on you at one time, but things just didn't work out for us. It was just as well, because I married a lovely lady and we had six wonderful children. Life was good to us until last year when she suddenly took a stroke and died. I couldn't stand living in the house without her, and I'm a lousy cook, so I moved here. You are the last person in the world I ever expected to see again."

Wheels were furiously turning in her mind. Who could this man possibly be? He seemed to know her, yet she only dated one man in her life and that was Willie . . . and Steven Pointer. She gazed into his unblemished face and recollections hit her. Yes, it was him . . . handsome, dignified, polite, and a gentleman. She took a deep breath and said, "Honey, have you ever had a toboggan ride on the seat of your pants?" They both laughed and hugged and laughed again.

"Life does play tricks on us sometimes, doesn't it?" he said with a chuckle. "Don't feel bad. I saw your toboggan load roll off the track and I watched you walk away with a man at your side. Something told me at that moment, I lost you for good. I met up with some old friends that night, and they drove me home. One of those girls became my wife."

"We have so much to catch up on," Steven said. "Let's take a walk in the garden. It's a lovely day and flowers are blooming. I want to hear where you've been and what you've done with your life."

They walked around the garden area, admiring all the beauty surrounding them, then sat on a bench in front of a beautiful flowing fountain, and became thoughtfully silent. Steven reached over and picked a 'Forget-me-not' and placed it in her hand, then held it between both of his, and the warmth flowed through them.

"I'm happy life has brought us together again," he said, with a twinkle in his eye.

"Me too," she whispered softly.

"Tell me all about your life Jessie. I can't wait to hear your story. I'm sure it's interesting."

She took a deep breath and gazed into the dancing waters in the fountain for several thoughtful moments before she spoke.

"My dear, dear friend, some of my past life is much too painful to recall, and is best forgotten, for everyone's sake. I buried all my disappointments and pain deep down in my memory vault, and threw the key away.

You watched me slide down a slippery slope, and my friend, I kept on slipping and sliding for many painful years thereafter. I can't share everything that happened in my life, but I'll tell you some of the interesting experiences I fought my way through. Just keep holding my hand, and hold on to your hat! The story of my life goes like this . . .

"I married an alcoholic. Oh, I didn't do it intentionally...."

GLOSSERY

<u>Jessie McGann and Willie Masterson - Main Characters</u>

<u>William and Mary Masterson – Willie's parents</u>

Archie – Willie's brother

Billy Masterson – Jessie and Willie's son

Captain Conrad – captain of the freighter, Lady Leeside

Dave and Evangeline Allendale – good friends of Jessie and Willie

David and Marth McGann – Jessie's parents

Doctor Zabbinski – Jessie's maternity doctor

Dolly and Grant Donahue – Jessie's sister and brother-in-law

Frederick Hammerfield – Sandy's second husband

Geoffrey and Katelyn Goodall – Jessie and Willie's neighbors

Gregory McGann – Jessie's brother

Henry and Helen Townsend – residence on Hogan's Isle

Jeannie – Jessie's co-worker

Joan Masterson – Willie's sister

Judy – Jessie's girlfriend

Kevin Fitzgibbon– Sandy and Randy's son

Lenny Goodall – Jessie's neighbor's son

Martin Masterson – Willie's distant cousin

Mr. and Mrs. Helper who rescued Sandy

Mr. Blackhart – tenant

Pete – kind hearted garage man

Randy Fitzgibbon– Sandy's first husband

Ray McGann – Jessie's brother

Rev. Fairweather – Pastor at Seagull landing

Rob Cruckshank – business man, valued customer, employer

Sandy Masterson – Jessie and Willie's daughter

Shelley – Billy Masterson's wife

FICTICIOUS PLACES

BATTLESHIP BAY – COUNTRY HOSPITAL, 50 MILES FROM CRITTER CREEK

CRITTER CREEK – WHERE THE COTTAGE WAS LOCATED

HARBOURVILLE – BOATING HARBOUR

HOGAN'S ISLE – A PORT IN A STORM

HOOTERVILLE – NAME GIVEN TO THE COTTAGE

HUDSON HOUSE – OUTPOST

MAGESTIC POINT – FISH CAMP ON LAKE WINNIPEG

MOODY MOUNTAIN – LOCATION OF PENITENTARY

SADDLE CREEK – WHERE GRANDMA LIVED

SEAGULL LANDING – FISHING STATION

WATTERTON – SMALL COUNTRY TOWN - STOPOVER

CPSIA information can be obtained
at www.ICGtesting.com
Printed in the USA
LVOW12s0106160218
566808LV00001B/44/P